Remnants: The Corporate Chronicles

Book One: Leaving the Nest

Lilliana Annette

Deeters

i

Dedication:

I would like to dedicate this book to my loving mother and father who, through all my mental and emotional turbulence, never once left my side. Thank you so much and always remember, no matter how much of a pain I am to you, I will always love you.

Also, to my friends, who are much like family and siblings to me. For without your support, this book would have never been possible! Thank you all so much and Blessed Be!

Contents

Lilliana Annette Deeters

iii

Acknowledgments

I'd like to take this time to say that a lot of this story's inspiration came from the table top RPG Shadowrun. Though I have not used any of their information due to copyright laws, those of you who have played the game of Shadowrun will notice similarities. I was sure to change any names of people or terms so as to not steal any of their ideas. I also want you to know the story itself as well as the characters are all originals. As well as this story is a work of fiction. Any similarities to any people, places, events that are happening, have happened or MAY happen both living, dead, or undead is completely coincidental.

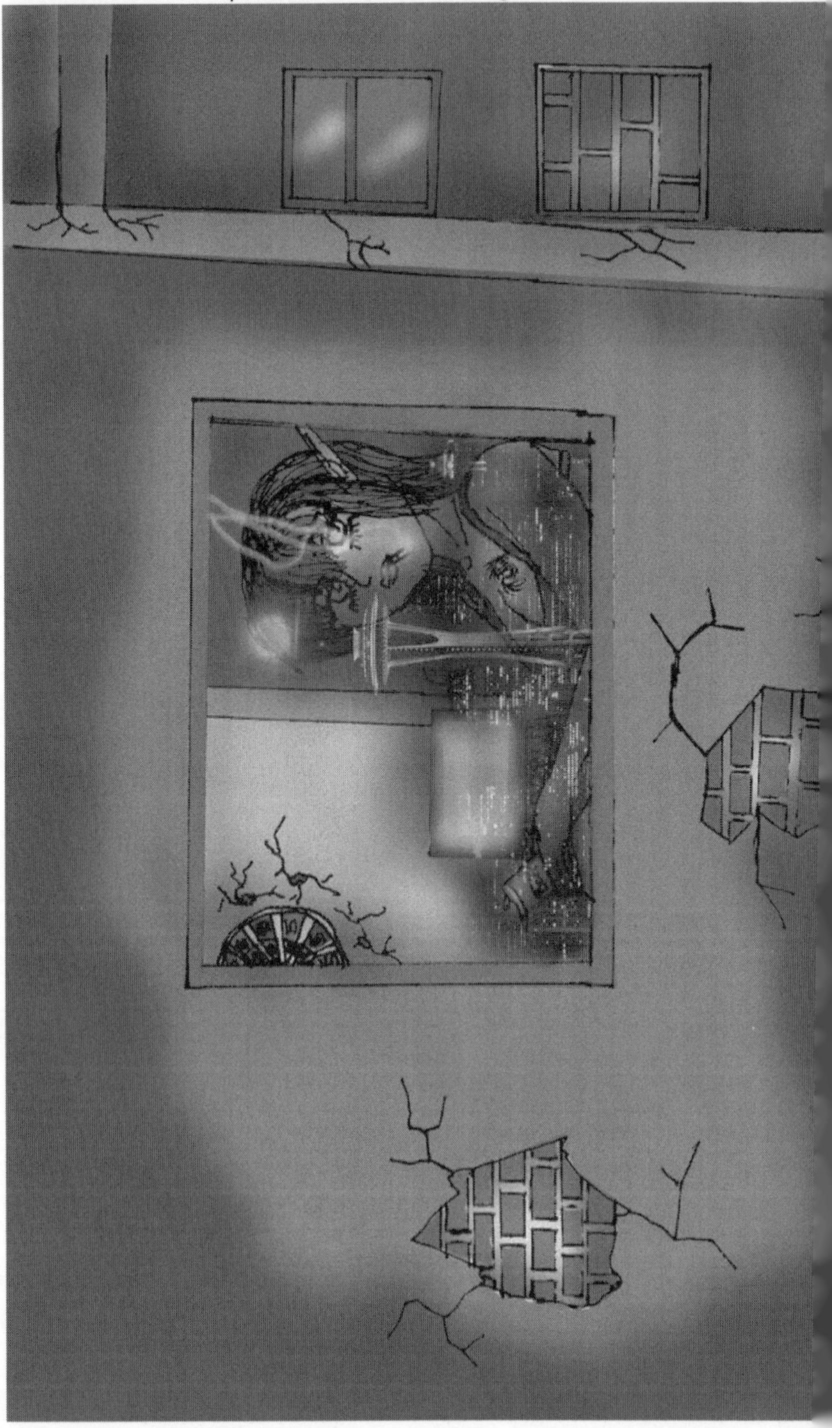

Lilliana Annette Deeters

Prelude to the Storm

July 1st 2060, New Seattle, Redmond Barrens
District 12.

20:14:00pm.

Did you ever have a dream? A dream that you
were worth more than what the world says you
are? That you had a greater purpose in life? I do
all the time, I just never thought much of it till
recently though. Here in New Seattle, you're
either a corporate worker, a no-name civilian....or
you're a Runner. And me you ask? Where do I
fit into all of this? Well, I work with guns, just
about any type of gun I know how to fire it, take it
apart, alter it, and put it back together better than
ever before. But other than being a spineless
engineer for Atlas Macro-technologies, there's no
work for someone like me. Besides, the corps
tried to wipe me out before. They got my entire
family, or so that's what I thought, but I'm getting
ahead of myself here. Perhaps I should start at
beginning; my name...Is Raven Destiny and this is
my story.

I had a good life, or so that's the way the MIN
records said it was. I found that to be a little
strange considering the fact that I was trained by
someone, somewhere, in my life to be able to take
apart guns and to kick through solid brick walls.
I don't quite recall where all these skills came

from. So, somewhere in my life there must have been a need for the ability to defend myself. But anyway, after the corps attacked my home, I was found somewhere outside Tir'Na'nOg unconscious. The only thing I could remember was part of my name, Raven. So, after I recovered in the hospital I was released into New Seattle to get a job. Yeah right! What a bunch of ~~flicking~~ bullshit! There aren't any jobs for half brain dead elf with skills in nothing but guns and martial arts. Accept being a Runner. So, I decided I'd make a living and get my revenge all in one day's work. Tch, boy was I naive! I'll tell you something friend, being a Runner ain't all fun and games. It's a lot of work and a lot of heart ache. Once I was released on "good behavior", I rented a small apartment in the Redmond Barrens, District 12 area. It wasn't anything extravagant, actually this area is a dumping ground for shit Runners like me. 5000 credits a month is pretty cheap though, and it was all I needed. A place to sleep, keep my brews and work on guns in my off time. I gave my fixer, Chip a call. He was a little dwarf guy, Decker by trade, and he usually got some decent runs.

"This is Chip, talk to me!" Chip's furry wrinkled face appeared on my video phone screen. I could never tell the age of a dwarf. To me they all looked like middle aged men with big bushy beards, small eyes and huge bulbous noses. Chip was no different in this aspect, he was supposed to be around his 20's, but to me he

looked like his was in his late 30's early 40's.
Yeah, call me racist if you want, but that's just my
opinion on dwarves as a whole. I've heard Chip
say similar, however, about elves like me though.

"Hey Chip, this is Raven. Ya got any jobs for
me?" Chip scratched his beard which looked like
some kind of a Fu-Man-Chu thing going on there.
He seemed kind of leery about giving me a job.
But he finally gave me an answer after a few
moments.
"Yeah, I got one, but I dunno if you're up for it."
He finally replied with a great deal of reserve.
"Oh yeah? Gimmie a shot! I bet I'll impress you."
I was always cocky and sure of myself. If there
was one thing in my life I could never do was give
up.
"Alright then, Chip replied as he tapped at his
deck, "I got a job for you. You heard of
Brackhaven Investments?" Of course I'd heard of
them, but since the corps had wiped out my
family and a part of my memory, I didn't have all
the details, so I just said I had no clue. "Well,
Brackhaven Investments is one of the biggest
investment corps in Seattle. Well, I'm looking for
a little bit of extra cred for a new cyber deck I had
my eye on. And well, business ain't working out
for shit right now, if ya know what I mean?"

"How much ya look'n to get off of them?" I
was curious. The more money the more trouble I
was gonna have to go through. Plus the more
money I was gonna negotiate for on this run.
Considering I thought it was gonna be a solo run.

"Well, I'm think'n about a 100 thou." He said it like he was ask'n me to borrow a single cred.

"A hundred thousand creds?! Holy ~~fuck~~ Chip, you know how hard that's gonna be? Consider'n the fact that I'm NOT a frigg'n Decker like you?!" I thought he was talk'n more around the lines of a thou or something in that area. But a hundred thousand credits?! That's a difficult task even for someone like me. "And furthermore, how much is my cut of this run? I mean, this is a lot of work for one person."

"I had a feeling you wouldn't be up for it. I got a smaller escort job for ya, if that's more your speed?" Chip smirked, he knew that would just piss me off because I loved a challenge and I hated being a ~~fucking~~ baby sitter for some corp jockey that needed help getting from place to place just to make illegal deals.

~~"Piss off you fucking halfer!"~~ Using a racial slur on someone who's supposed to be giving you your next job isn't exactly a smart thing, but I was pissed! I was just getting ready to hang up on him when he chimed in with a more serious tone. "Alright alright! Geez Raven you fly off the handle too quick! Look, I got someone to help ya out." I smirked, I knew he'd see it my way if I just pitched a big enough fit. Chip got decent runs, but he didn't like to hire on a lot of help for the jobs he got. So sometimes you had to piss and moan at him to get him to make the extra effort. "That's more like it. Who is he? He better be good cause I ain't baby sitt'n no new-bee ass hole when I could be getting the job done. And ya still haven't told me how much my cut is."

"SHE, Chip corrected me, is a decker named Crystaleen. One of
the best I know, next to me of course."

"Oh of course!" I added in with the utmost sarcasm. Yeah chip was good, but he wasn't exactly the best of the best. I had heard stories of a decker by the name of Shadow that could jack into anything and basically ruled the net. As far as I was concerned, until you were that good, you didn't have any room to talk.

"And she's a pretty bad ass fighter too." He added, knowing that if they couldn't keep up with me in a fight, there was no way I was going to work with them.

"I'll give you her digits and you guys can set up the meet. As for your cut. How's 25 sound?"

"That better be 25 thousand. And it better be a piece! I don't much feel like hav'n to split my cut with someone I've never laid eyes on, especially when the only info I got on her skill is hear-say." I had learned in my life not to trust anyone. Especially not in this corp war ridden world we lived in today."

"Yes Raven, that's twenty-five thousand credits a piece. Would I make you split your share with someone you didn't even know?" He was trying to sound all sincere and giving and shit. "I'm hurt Raven, I thought we knew each other better than that?"

"Cut the crap Chip! I'll take the job. Forward me Crystaleen's digits and I'll give her a call. Once I get the money I'll cred your account, same as always."

"Alright! Happy doing business with you Raven!" Chip seemed rather happy as he forwarded me Crystaleen's number and signed off. He should be, the little halfer bastard was getting 50 thousand credits just for sitting ~~on his ass~~ doing nothing, while two girls went out and caused a ruckus. If I didn't need the money, on any other occasion, I would have never risked the chances. The negatives far out-weighed the positives on this one. Working with a runner I didn't know from Adam, stealing a large sum of money in one large amount in one go, and doing it all for a fixer I just met two days ago. Oh well, I was going need some money to make rent and to start buying supplies for refitting my guns or anyone else's that became a contact. So this was my best bet at starting out. I figured it was make or break time. Float or sink, fight or flight. This was it, this was the moment.

I dialed up this chick named Crystaleen, I really didn't know what to expect, but I was kind of impressed to hear about another female Runner out there. One that was good anyway, and not a ~~fucking~~ twit or a whore. In these days, a lot of girls chose to find an easy out through the corps one way or another. It was sad really. Not that I can blame them in the long run, this was not the glamorous life that you dreamt about when you're in your room at night at your folks' place thinking about boy bands and pretty pink ponies. This sure as hell is no life for a "pretty princess". When she finally picked up she kept her video off. A lot of runners did that these days, with the corporate phone taps and all, you could never be too careful these days.

"What do you want!?" A very cold but smooth and feminine woman's voice met my ears. I was honestly kind of startled one of the first times I was actually at a loss for words. "This is Raven," I replied. My voice was cracked and I felt like a new-bee. The sad truth of the matter was, that for as much shit as I talked, and for as good as my skills were, I was nothing but a new-bee at this too.   Crystal still didn't turn on her visuals, but she continued to speak without the use of them. She probably was still unsure of me.   I can't blame her much though.

"Yeah so? What do you want with me?"

    "I'm your runner for this mission." I tried very hard to get my head out my ass and pull it together. I had to make her believe I wasn't as green as I actually was. So I hardened my voice and acted like I was pissed off that she was asking me all these questions.

"Who gave you my contact information?"   She asked, with a sharp resonance in her voice.

"Chip, a fixer go through, gave me your digits. I'm the gun-slinger specialist he talked about. Me an you are supposed to go do this job for him over at Brackhaven Investments? I needed a decker to help me break into the systems." I could only hope that Chip had told her the mission specs. He had been known to forget to fill in both sides of the party on what the hell they were doing.

"Oh okay!" Her voice softened, though it still maintained sense of cold to it. The visual came up and I was startled to see what was looking back at me from the other side. A very young curvaceous blue haired Elvin decker. She was all done up in blue biker digs, her hair was long, it stopped about the middle of her back and was naturally wavy. Her eyes were as well a blue-ish color, and, almost looked like they were small pools of semi-frozen blue liquid. Her skin was also an eerie off-blue color. Where her skin was naturally pale it also maintained a blue tint like she was frozen. I figured as well as the data jack which was an obvious protrusion from her temple, she possessed some magical ability. A deck-mage was a rare find. Most mages didn't care for cyber ware, as it drained their essence; the body's natural energy which was used to cast spells. Yeah, I read about it in some goofy gamer geek site when I was net surfing one day when I was bored. "Yes, she continued, you can't be too careful these days with the corp wars and all. I don't discuss business over the phone. Meet me at the crime mall in 1 hour. Come alone and don't be late!" She began to sign off without another word. I tried to ask her for more info but she was already gone

"Wow, what a ~~fucking~~ bossy bitch!" I said to myself as I got my gear together and my modified Desert Eagle.
"Well, looks like we're about to find out just how good this chick really is. I got into my car, which was an old beat up piece of crap Sundance.
"~~God damn it~~ how I hate Plymouth! They suck!" I complained as it took me several tried to get the ~~damn~~ piece of shit to start! Once I got it going, I started down the road. For once the roads were pretty clear. I figured most of the people were out attending

the annual summer festival that was held in main park in downtown Seattle every year around this time. The people of this city were like androids...machines! Created hollow dolls and puppets, designed to move about the city autonomously; completing monotonous and remedial every-day tasks. The drone of the traffic...the eternal hum of street lamps and neon signs. The cold...gray dark plas-create street and walk ways. Colorless, lifeless cement walls. It was all…so disgusting! I had come to put up and deal with a lot of things in this world. But there were two things that I found absolutely un-fucking-tolerable! And those were idiots and machines! I fucking couldn't stand them! But, to exist in this dark shadowy hell, this concrete underworld of shadow and hypocrisy, you had to put up with both idiots and machines...all of them...some more so than others. The cybered out freaks that roamed the streets, half dead to the world...their essence drained by the cold titasteel, carbon fiber that laced their bodies.

Like phantoms they moved through the street as I drove, dark and lifeless automatons. I pray that I may never become that way...that I may never become the disgusting abominations they are. Half human half machine, living but not living, existing only to cause pain and destruction. It was a fucking shadow of life. Not one that I wanted and I sure as hell had no respect for anyone that chose it for themselves! My radio antenna was busted, so the only music I could really get was some ~~fucking~~ gospel ~~shit~~. Which only added to my growing aggravation. I reached into my jacket pocket for my pack of cigarettes; I only had 3 left.

"Looks like we're going to have to get this night over with quickly." I said quietly to myself, as I turned down an alley, the meeting point was just at the other end. I passed a group of troll gang members harassing a young Elvin prostitute. I knew what would happen next: A dark alley, three trog gangers and one little dandelion eater hoe. Yeah...I was an elf too so why didn't I stop to help my own? Well, I sure as hell didn't like it...but it wasn't my concern...none of this was. That wasn't the way the world worked these days. "No good comes without consequence." I said to myself as I just drove on by. It was something that had become my mantra these days.

Whenever I had tried to help people and change things for the better, I just got myself fucked for

it! And not in any form of a good way either.
They would have their way with her and she'd end
up dead in a dumpster somewhere. The police
would take one look and say;
"This case is going to be a tough one."   But truly,
on the inside they were saying; "That's one less
piece of street trash that we have to clean up."

    STAR was the local police force, and they
were as crooked as the corp heavy weights. As I
said before, this was the world of corporate
corruption and sin that I lived in. And none of
this was my concern, it didn't matter...none of this
mattered. Only the fire on the end of my cigarette
and the black viper that was in my head lights...it
was my contact for this job. None of this
mattered,
just this job..and the payment. My trigger finger
was twitching and I could feel a storm coming.
This was just the prelude!

Chapter 1

The Shadow Calls

April 2nd 2060, New Seattle Redmond Barrens,
District 12
00:11:23 AM.

The black Viper in front of me was definitely
Crystal's car, and it was a beautiful car at that. As
I drove up she stepped out of her car, she was
amazing really. Her hair was done up in the
traditional Japanese top knot that most samurai
had. She had pins in her hair and a rather
interesting outfit. It wasn't quite, "Traditional",
like the rest of her outfit was. I figured she had
obviously changed clothes since I spoke to her.
She wore a dark blue, almost purple tight leather
mini skirt, that she buckled by a belt which started
high on her right hip, and ran down about 4 inches
from her left hip bone which was covered by the
skirt. I figured the belt was just for show. Her skin
was still pale and tinted slightly blue like I had
seen in the video phone screen. I didn't bother
about asking why, and not just because it would
have been frigging rude, but because on her back
she had a HUGE ice blue katana.

"Are you her?" She asked vaguely. I knew
the ropes of this biz, just not all the techniques.
She didn't want to just come out and ask if i was a
runner. That was hired to do an illegal job. Good
way to get a bullet in your head. "Yeah, I
responded with similar vagueness, "I'm Raven,
your contact

Lilliana Annette Deeters

for this job. I take it you're Crystal?" Just as I got the name out of my mouth she had the tip of the blade up to my throat. I didn't even see her pull it! She was fast! Really fast! I was definitely impressed. I would have only been more impressed if her gun draw was as fast. I tried very hard not to show my fear but I think she saw the small sweat drop run down the side of my face. "Don't EVER call me Crystal!" Her voice cut across me like a shrill arctic wind. "That name is reserved for friends and loved ones! You will call me Crystaleen till further notice! You get me!?" "Yeah, I get you." I said again failing at trying to remain calm.

"Your look of fear says it all. But," she sheathed the sword very skillfully onto her back while maintaining her entire focus on me, "I wanted to hear you say it for yourself". For a moment, I just stood there completely and utterly stunned. I wasn't quite sure what to make of Crystaleen at first. The woman just fucking held a blade to my throat! Do you THINK I was happy about that? I was frigging furious! On any other occasion, I'd have told her to fuck off and taken my business elsewhere, if I didn't put a fucking bullet in her god-damned head for that! But I needed the money, and I didn't have the slightest clue where the hell I would find another Decker willing to take on this mission on such short notice. "So, I said, trying to break the ice, you know where this place is where we gotta do this job at?"

"It's just downtown, she replied, pointing in the general direction of downtown Seattle. You can jack into the machines from any location. But I'm willing to bet you an evening in my bed that the best way to get what we're looking for is going straight through their mainframe." She shot me a coy grin and I wasn't sure, but I was thinking she was coming on to me there. Hell if I cared at this point though. Till we got this job done she could make all the lesbian advances on me she wanted. I wasn't about to fuck this up just because this chick thought that I was into that stuff. So I figured I'd let it go for now.

"Alright, I said, unwittingly not knowing that I just agreed to her bargain, you got a plan?"

I wanted to make sure we were going to be going into this with some kind of plan. Preferably a plan A, B, and a C. But if not, at least ONE plan of some reasonable sense. Crystal smiled as she tightened the sash that held her sword to her back and crossed over her shoulder and down between her rather supple breasts which were almost visible through the very low cut light blue leather top she wore.

"I think I might have an idea". She said, once more, looking around again to see if there was anyone listening in on our conversation. She then moved closer to me and I tilted my head a bit to listen to her plan.

"Alright, we'll drive to the Brackhaven main office in downtown. I'll let you out two blocks up the road from the building. I'll have you scout the perimeter around the main building, to see how the security in the area is. Once you've figured out how tight security is, contact me using this two way radio." Crystal handed me a small ear piece that had a small wire that came down along the jaw line near the mouth. It was similar to what secret service agents would have worn only smaller and more difficult to detect. I could only imagine where she got it.

"I'll jack into the main system from outside the building, from there, I'll cause the security systems to shut down momentarily. Then, using the information you've given me on the security around the building, we'll get inside and hit the mainframe from there. Simple isn't it?" Yeah it sounded simple enough in words, but if there was one thing I had learned in the short time I was in this "profession", it was that nothing was ever that simple in this world.

"Alright, one question though." I said, tilting my head toward hers more with a very cynical glance. "What's the question?" She asked in response." "Why am *I* the one that has to risk my neck trying to figure out security?" I still cringe when I think about this job to this day!

"Uhm because you're the new-bee, DUH!" She chuckled and with that she opened her car door and slid into the driver side. She disappeared behind dark tinted windows. I started to open my car door and the handle fell off. *"What a fucking piece of shit!"* I thought to myself. Sadly, no matter how hard I tried, I couldn't get the frigging door to open! So, in my irritated state, I gave the car door a swift kick. I left a boot imprint on the door and I actually shifted the car slightly. Unfortunately, the only thing I managed to accomplish was making my driver's side car door fall right off its hinges. *"That fucking figures!"* I thought to myself, I finally get a decent job and my car falls apart. I slid in and tried to start the car but it wasn't working for me. It sputtered and spit and just made me feel even more green than Crystal had already made me feel. In fact, I think I was feeling so green I was turning red and it wasn't from anger. Crystal let her window slowly lower and looked over at me. "Having some car troubles there Raven?" She snickered under her breath as she asked. *"Fuck you, you fucking rich bitch!"* I thought to myself as I heard her snicker at her own snide comment. Even though she tried to hide her snickers, I still heard them. We elves have amazingly good hearing. Especially when someone's bad mouthing us.

"Yeah, I replied, feeling quite heated at this point. "This fuck'n piece of ~~shit god-damned~~ cock sucking car won't start!" I could cuss like a sailor when I got going.

"If it's not one thing its fifteen fucking others!" By the tone of my voice Crystal could tell that I was obviously embarrassed and pissed off.

Sadly...she caught the embarrassed part more than the pissed off part.

"Ah, ya poor thing. Crystal said in the most non-sympathetic and sarcastic voice I think I've ever heard in my life. "Ya wanna ride? It'll only cost you an extra five percent." She smirked as she just screwed me out of at least 500 credits.

"You bloody gutter snipe bitch! I HATE being ripped off! You would CHARGE your own partner a cut of her earnings jus to give her a ride!? YOU ARE SUCH A ~~FUCKING~~ BITCH!!!" I think I woke up half the neighborhood we were in. I distinctly remember hearing someone to tell me to "Shut the fuck up!" But I didn't care, I was too pissed off at Crystal at that moment that I could literally feel the vein in my forehead pulsing. So I could give a shit less who I was disturbing at the time.

"Yeah I know!" Was her only response as she just smiled at me through her window. "But if you want this job that bad, it's gonna cost ya. Call it a business expense if you will. I could always call Chip and tell him you changed your mind. I'm sure he'd be happy to give you a body guard job that you could just walk around on, since you don't have a car. After all I'm sure Chip could find me someone with reliable transportation to help me out on this run instead of you." I don't know what pissed me off more: The fact that if she made good on her little threat there that Chip WOULD actually take me off this job, or the fact that the bitch was snickering at me. All I knew was that she was REALLY pissing me off at that moment! *"You are a ~~fucking~~ evil, evil bitch! This is ~~god damn~~ fucking extortion! I'm not ~~fucking~~ paying you shit to ride in your ~~god damned~~ car!"*

But what other choice did I have? I HAD to get there and get the job done or I was going to be totally fucked for cash anyway. "......three percent." I said, grumbling and folding my arms over my chest as I leaned back against my pile O' shit with a childish huff.

"Four and a half"! She replied quickly.

"Four percent and not a damn credit more! You ~~fucking~~ greedy bitch!" I snapped at her, clenching my fists. I soo wanted to pulverize her right there and then. But that wouldn't be good for business. I think Crystal seen that I couldn't be pushed any further, so she just grinned and went from there.

"You drive a hard bargain Raven, but I think I can deal with that. Hop in!" I still wasn't any happier with her, but then this wasn't any time to be squabbling like school kids, or to be negotiating over pocket change. I hopped in the passenger's side and shut the door.

"Let's go then." Was the only thing I really said to her after that before she started down the road. We didn't' talk much during the drive. I spent most of my time polishing my Desert Eagle. It was really the only memory I had left of my past. That and the black dragon tattoo I had on my left breast. I think it was a family seal of some type I had assumed. But through all my searching I had yet to come up with the whereabouts in which the symbol originated. We slowly drove past the building and around the block a few times. I could tell she was casing the scene. The building was like any other corp fuck hole. Armed guards, mostly Atlas Knights, patrolling around. Some guys in suits who I didn't really recognize. They looked like they were young Asian men though. A lot of fake plants around the outside of the building. Most likely hiding automated machine gun turrets. Bastards like this loved to gun runners down before they even made it to the door.

Crystal was just about to pull up to the building.

"What the hell are you doing?!" I asked her in a loud but low tone. Didn't want to yell and give ourselves away.

"I'm parking the car; what the hell does it look like I'm doing?" She looked at me like I was insane. Maybe, you have to be a little bit insane to take on a job like this with a woman like her.

"Don't park here!" I said, surprised she hadn't noticed what I thought was the obvious. "Look, do you see those plants right there?" I asked her, pointing across her lap to a small group of shrubbery that, to me, looked completely and utterly fake.

"Yeah? She responded, still looking at me like was a few smokes short of a whole pack,

"What fucking relevance does that have to our

job?"

"They're fake." I replied simply. Apparently, she wasn't very fire-arms savvy. At least not when it came to the construction and de-construction of mounted and rotary machine gun types.

"Again, what the HELL does that have to do with this job?!" She responded, becoming noticeably irritated with my apparent obsession with these stupid fucking bushes.
"Look, she continued, if you're all into shrubbery and that shit like those country bumpkin elves, then that's fine. But, do me a favor and keep your head IN the game right now okay?!" She seemed to be getting to the point where she wanted to knock me through her passenger side window rather than continue this conversation. And I was getting annoyed that she couldn't see what I thought was a piss poor cover up job. "You don't get it do you?" I finally looked at her and started to explain:
"If they're fake, that means they don't have roots. Which means they're not actually IN the ground. Do you follow?" She looked at me blankly for a second before responding.
"No, not really." I smacked myself in the head with the palm of my hand and grumbled. "*I need a fucking cigarette!*"

"Look! I tried to explain it to her as simply and patiently as possible, lighting up a cigarette to calm my nerves. If those plants aren't rooted into the actual dirt on the ground, that means that there is most likely an automated gun turret under the plants! And look!" I pointed off to the side at a few more plants, more importantly, the large tree that was obviously fake which was probably housing a hidden rocket launcher inside of the fake trunk.

"That's probably some really BIG frigg'n gun! Jus wait'n for us to step out of this car and step onto the grounds of this place so they can blow our asses clear to fuck'n Mars!" She looked at me in surprise at first. As if she couldn't believe that this green new-bee runner figured all that out on her own. Then she gave me a good looking over, it wasn't too hard to figure out what I was good at.

I always wore pretty much the same thing. A black armored leather jacket that had seen its better days. It was faded, more gray now than black. Some of the ablative plating was beginning to show through the older more worn areas of the leather. My hair was short barely shoulder length and razor cut so it kept its style without much work on my part. What bit of make-up I wore was just some lip gloss to keep my lips from getting chapped. Who the fuck had time to do make-up these days anyway? My pants were really tight fit because they were actually some cheap pair I got from a rescue mission I had stopped at after getting out of the hospital. They didn't really fit me so I left them unbuttoned and unzipped. My hips and butt were actually shapely enough, for being an elf, to hold them up without worry. I wore some old faded camouflage combat boots that the strings looked like they had gotten eaten by something a long time ago. My boots had some armor plating on them too, but it was obvious that it had been put there years ago and very much out-of-date for the times.

I was clean, for the most part, but I always had some form of grease or power stains on my skin and clothes. And I smelt heavily of gun powder, oil and cigarette smoke. I always had at least two guns on me at all times. Namely, my modified Desert Eagle, and my berretta 9mm.

"Wow!" Crystal said with a new tone of amazement in her voice. "You figured all that out jus by glancing at it?! You're good!" She was indeed impressed.

"Well yeah, I'm a gunslinger specialist after all. Guns are kinda my thing, DuH! I could tell jus by the way the concrete separates around the plants that there was something down there. It's a really ingenious design though I must admit. The guns must be on a pivot, that allows the separation to look almost natural. The only problem is normal concrete is cut on a smaller angle. The angle in which they cut that concrete and the thickness of the blocks is the exact thickness needed to house about a 63 millimeter machine gun comfortably. If not for the pivot, the angle would have to have been even shorter, to allow room for the barrel to come out of the ground." Crystal looked at me for the longest time as if she was actually seeing the real me finally. I think that was the first time

Crystaleen thought of me as a partner rather than just a kid. It's kind of ironic really; all this time I was worried about baby-sitting some half-cocked hair brained action hero wanna-be new-bee, and it was my current partner that was the one doing the babysitting at first. I think that was the first and only thing Chip ever did right by hooking Crystal and me up on a team.

"That's actually very impressive Raven!" Crystal was amazed that I was that intelligent for such a young elf.
"Really? I didn't think it was that impressive. Seems like jus common sense to me." I had lost my memory after all. The skills I had were taught to me a long time ago. It was just second nature to me right now. She shook her head as she pulled into a dark alley a few blocks down the road.
"No way Raven! That's some serious military shit up there in that cute little burgundy head you got there! Where the hell did you learn that stuff?! That's like straight out of an Atlas Macrotech manual or sumthin!" I thought about what she had just said for a moment, everyone knew about Atlas Macro-technology in the world these days. It was only the world's largest leading manufacturer in both military and civilian weapons. Not to mention, ironically, the only corporation NOT in a corporate war with someone else...well...at least not back when this part of my story took place. But to me...Atlas corp was more than a gun seller. It held some kind of deep dark inner meaning to me...Like, when I heard

someone say "Atlas Macrotech", a little buzzer went off in my head. I just couldn't get to the thing making the buzzing sound.

"I dunno where I learned it." It was the only response I could give her. I could have lied and made up some crazy bad ass story, but I didn't have a good lie to tell at the time. She did a double take when I said I didn't know.
"What do you have amnesia or something?" I think the comment was originally meant to be a joke. Well, I didn't think it was very funny. In fact, it kind of hurt. But hell, what could I say really? She didn't know me from Jack!
"Yeah...I do…" Was my only response I had for her comment. I then opened the door and stepped out of her viper. I started to load my Desert Eagle and my 9mm Beretta. I was ready to go. Even if it just felt like someone stabbed me in the heart with a dull rusty spoon. As we stepped out, we ran around to the corner of the building and started around the back. She was fast! My god she could move like no one I had ever seen. She was to the back of the building and waiting to move on by the time I got to side. To this day, I've only ever met one other person who could move that fast. Once I caught up to her I whispered:

"So, what's the plan?" I was scanning the area as I screwed the silencer onto my Beretta. My Desert Eagle was too big for a silencer, so I only used it as a last resort. She knelt down a bit as she watched a man in a suit make rounds near the side of the building. "Think you can take that guy out quietly?" She asked me as she pushed her sword loose from its hilt just in case I fucked it all up. To trust me with a task like that this early I knew Crystal had to have some faith in my abilities. I hopped I didn't let her down as I answered, "Yeah, just try and keep up!" I slowly worked my way along the wall of the building, Beretta in hand, as I approached the suit from around the building. As I crept up behind him I got ready to put a bullet in the back of his head when suddenly he stopped. *"Ah fucking damn it!"* Thoughts raced through my head. *"Don't fucking tell me this suit just heard me sneaking up behind him!?"* I held my breath, waiting for him to move again. *"Just keep moving...keep moving, you fucking pencil dick!"* I froze, I wasn't sure what to do. He was looking back and forth as if he heard something. *"Bloody fucking hell! Don't fucking turn around!"* I kept thinking to myself, as my heart was beating so fast I was surprised he couldn't hear that. My palms were sweating and so was I! I felt sick and white. My knees were weak and, as far as I could remember, I had never actually killed someone before. Not with them facing me anyway. *"If this guy turns around, I'm going to have to shoot him. And I don't know if I can do that looking right at him."* I was scared to death, every second felt like a fucking eternity to me. Then slowly, he continued forward. I felt the knot in the pit of my stomach slowly unwind. I exhaled, shuddering a little, feeling my heart beat return to a normal pace. I looked back, Crystal had her sword pulled and ready to leap. My god I didn't even hear her move! Would she have really killed that guy for me? Or was she going to take us both down?

I didn't really have time to try and figure it out. As the suit took a step forward, I pointed my Beretta at the back of his head and squeezed the trigger. The bullet discharged quietly as they do when silenced, for a moment his body stood there motionless before a thin line of blood started to run down the back of his head from the small bullet hole that the 9 mm shell had left in his head. I watched as the thin line trickle down and stain the collar of his white shirt, his body shuddered and just fell over. Killing someone in real life looks nothing like it does in the movies. When someone dies in the movies and in trideo-sims, they do this whole cool twirling thing, or they at least have a cool phrase they let out before they die. In real life, it doesn't look anything like that. It just seems like everything disappears below their waist, and they seem like they really don't realize what just happened. Then THUD! They're laying on the ground in a puddle of their own blood. They say a piece of you dies when you take the life another. Well, Its true! Very, very true. When that suit hit the ground, I felt suddenly, a little colder inside. Like a piece of me just kind of disappeared with his life. As I slid the suit back away from the corner of the building back by Crystal, I realized just how frigging heavy dead weight can really be. Guy couldn't have been more than 150lbs. But dead, this fucker felt like he weighed a ton. Oh, and on the part about movies and dead people, they also don't mention the part where when someone dies, that they shit themselves!

It stinks something awful! Suit must of had spicy curry or something for dinner. Crystal smiled at me in her half grin way and simply said, "Nice, a little sloppy, but effective. I really thought he was gonna turn around there for a second! But he didn't so you got off easy on that one." I was still obviously a little pale. The color hadn't quite   returned to my skin yet.
"Yeah, for a moment there, so did I!" I said laughing about it now as I breathed a sigh of relief. Then Crystal looked at me seriously as she tossed me the suit's Ingram sub-machine gun.
"What would you have done if he did?" She gave me the most serious look she had ever given me as she re- sheathed her sword. I thought about it for a long moment. Actually playing the scenario over in my mind. And, for what seemed like forever to me, I couldn't answer her. But she continued to look at me, as if having the patience of a teacher. Finally I looked up at her and simply said,
".....to be honest, I really don't know." I felt like a moron, but it was the truth. For some reason I just felt I could be honest with her. She simply smiled and said, "That's what I thought."   She hid the body in the shadows and started around the side of the building with her deck in hand.

I put everything that had just happened out of

my mind for now I really didn't have the time or the concentration to focus on morality or what ifs right now. I needed to get into position for the next phase of the plan. Crystal wouldn't be there to bail my dumb ass out if I screwed up this time. *"Time to get focused!"* I told myself, as I moved into position and waited for her signal.

Chapter 2
The Shadows Call Pt. 2

July 2nd 2060 New Seattle
Downtown Neo-Seattle Brackhaven Investments
Main Building

01:04:09AM.

As Crystaleen rounded the side of the building, there was another suit near the outside computer terminal. Yeah, big corps and a lot of other public buildings have these terminals built into their walls on the outside. They kind of look like old ATM machines from back in the 21st century. Only they aren't just used to make credit withdrawls in my world. They can also be used to make video-phone calls, look up information, or even access the network. Isn't the cyber age grand? They are typically favorite hang outs for Deckers like Crystaleen. Mostly because Deckers can use these terminals to jack into computer systems remotely. And you thought the internet was complex? She rounded the corner and motioned for me to wait. She moved so fast around the building, behind the suit and had him by his neck with his mouth covered. She pulled him into the shadows and with quick flick of her wrists she broke his neck! I was amazed to say the least, and a little frightened too! She was A

LOT better than I gave her credit for. As she drug the guy back into the shadows and disarmed him of his gun and clips, I meekly made my way over to her.

"Well...that was...not bad." Yeah right Raven! I really sounded sooo unimpressed right there. I was thoroughly impressed and horrified at the same time. I could barely get the knot out my throat! Crystal laughed and smiled up at me. "Yeah I thought you might be surprised when you saw my how fast I moved. I'm not the fastest, but I've got a good bit of speed on in me." She returned her attention to the perimeter. *"Not the fastest!?"*

I thought to myself, Jesus this chick could probably take out just about any runner I had ever heard of or spoken to. And I had heard some stories about a lot of them, but spoken to only a handful. I was still in the afterglow of what she had done, so I didn't see Crystal get up and move. I actually jumped when she yelled to me.
"Raven! c'mon let's go!" She called to me. She was about twelve feet from me already. I didn't realize I had been day dreaming for that long. I cautiously made my way over to her.
"So, what's the plan?" I asked quietly as I looked about It was hard to keep the SMG hidden when all I had was a light ballistics jacket. The coast seemed to be clear for the most part, other than the normal security guards looming about. Crystal looked around one last time then whispered in my ear.

"Alright, I'm gonna jack into the terminal. Keep watch and make sure no one interrupts. I'm defenseless in the physical world when I'm jacked into the network." I nodded to her;

"No problem Crystaleen. Jus do whatcha gotta do and I'll take care of the rest out here. I won't let them touch you." I pulled my Beretta out of its holster and kept watch over the perimeter. Crystal put her deck down in front of her and plugged it into a cord that connected to another jack which she plugged into the terminal in front of her. Which in turn, was plugged directly into her skull. I saw her eyes go blank. It was the first time I had honestly seen a Decker jack into something. Kind of disturbing at first glance. It was like watching someone's soul be sucked from their body. Her eyes...they were just… vacant. The only thing that moved were her hands. I couldn't' even imagine what it was like back then.

"Ick! I'm definitely NEVER getting one of THOSE put into my skull! That's kinda creepy!" So I said, but at the same time, it was amazing watching her work. I continued to watch diligently, however. This was my first time on a real job, and I wasn't going to screw this up! As I watched the guards make their rounds, completely oblivious to what was going on right beside the building, I suddenly heard movement by the main entrance of the building. These huge elf ears weren't just used to frame my skull! I spun around and seen two men coming out of the building looking in our direction. They were particularly interested in Crystaleen who was still jacked into the system! "Fucking hell!" I cussed to myself. "She must have tripped a silent alarm in the system or some weird nerdy-ass tech bull shit like that!

They were strange looking guys: They were dressed in red armor and they had green cyber eyes both of them. At their sides they carried two swords, katanas by the look of them, much like Crystal's. One was a long blade, about the same length as the one on Crystal's back, and the other was about a foot shorter. They also had subs strapped to their back.

"Time to see how useful this Ingram really is!" I said, with great vigor, as I swung the gun around and opened fire on the armored men. No sooner did the bullets start flying than did the two of them start moving! They were as fast as Crystal if not faster! The one jumped over me while the other jumped up and ran along the side of the building toward me. Maybe a more experienced runner would have been able to figure this trick out, but I was still pretty green at the time. I couldn't shoot them both, so as the one landed behind me, the one running along the building kicked the gun from my hands and the one behind me took my legs out from under me.

As I hit the ground, the SMG went skidding somewhere away from me. I had heard of these guys before. They were the infamous Crimson Sword! A group of heavily cybered street samurai that sold their skills to the highest bidders. They were usually contracted out to do high end mercenary work or to guard big time corporate CEOs when they were doing work in dangerous areas. So what the fuck were they doing here at Brackhaven!? The rumor was that one of these guys could take down a whole group of highly trained and highly skilled runners. *"Just my fucking luck!"* I got stuck fighting with two of the bastards! As soon as I hit the ground, the one who kicked the gun out of my hands had his sword drawn and was about to run me through! Damn these guys were too fast! Just then, I heard the other guy behind me draw his blade. As I said, good ears! I knew I was dead if I didn't move and move now! But what could I do? There was no-where to move to! I'd never be able to pull a gun fast enough to shoot both of them!

Then it just hit me, like someone in my brain was telling me exactly what to do. *"Roll ya dumb dandelion eat'n bitch! Use your martial arts!"* I rolled out of the way of the one who was going to stab me and to the side. It forced the other to reposition himself. Giving me just enough time to spin around on my back and up onto my hands. I then pushed up off of my hands, sending my legs straight upward. As I shot up, I thrust my heels into the face of the samurai that was behind me. I felt flesh and bone shatter and give under the pressure, speed, and force of the kick. I could hear the metal and carbon fiber of the samurai's cyber ware fold, bend and snap under my foot. I twisted my body into a spin while my body rose up. I felt his armor crumple under the torque of my powerful legs. While air born, I shoved the broken man away with my legs and flipped to right myself in the air and landed on my feet.

"That's gonna leave a mark!" I said with a smug grin as watching him twitch momentarily on the ground. However, I barely got the sentence out of my mouth before the one that was now behind me closed the gap. He ran his blade right through my left shoulder, it pierced right through even the hardened leather and plating of my jacket. I felt the sting of the cold sharp metal as it bit deep into my arm, rendering it utterly useless. I screamed and was quickly floored by the rather large and swift sock in the jaw I got from that sneak attack. "I thought samurai were supposed to be honorable?" I hissed and spit, rather unimpressed by a rear attack as I ripped the blade from my shoulder which was an unwise decision on my part. I thought I was going to vomit! *"That hurt more than the fucking stab!"* The shock and blood loss was beginning to make me woozy. The samurai said something to me in Japanese, which to this day, I still don't know what the hell he said, and slowly started to make his way over to me.

To make things worse, the one that I thought I killed was started to move again.
"God damn cyber zombies!" I cussed at them as I pulled myself to my feet. I couldn't' move my left

arm, and it was going numb, it felt like it wasn't even connected to me anymore. I was left with only one arm to deal with two bad ass samurai guys. I wasn't about to quit now though! If I did, Crystal was a goner for sure. Luckily, they hadn't taken my legs out yet. Very sloppy on their part, considering I crushed the one's face with a single kick last time. I got ready, these guys were already more than a match for me and now I was fighting handicapped. I waited for their move. The one was still at full strength. The only thing he was missing was his long sword. He would be harder to take on at close range considering his other blade was shorter and faster to swing. The other guy's face was all fucked up but he still had both swords and neither one had drawn their gun yet. It was the proverbial rock and a hard place rule. *"Fuck me! "*

The still healthy, but down to one sword guy, moved first. The bastard was so frigging fast. I couldn't keep up with him being as hurt as I was so I took another on the cheek for it. Then a kick to the mid-section and another foot to the head. My ears were ringing and I was seeing double now as I stumbled backwards ready to fall over. I felt someone catch me in mid fall and at first I thought it was Crystal. Then I felt the agonizing sting in my left shoulder as the hamburger faced samurai pulled my arms back behind me into a full nelson. I screamed in pain as I felt my shoulder gushing blood. It was running down the front of my chest. The white tank top I had on was now stained almost completely red and I threw up all over my boots. I yelped in agony, feeling the muscles and tendons rip but that was a short lived breath, as another fist came into my jaw twice then swift knee to my stomach again. I puked blood as the one behind me let me drop to the ground. I fell into the puddle of my own blood and sick barely able to keep myself conscious.

They started chattering to each other in Japanese again. It was probably something along the lines about how pathetic I was and wondering if I was more useful in bed or something stereotypical of Japanese men. I couldn't understand the language to begin with, coupled with the fact that my head was pounding and my ears were ringing. I was also having increasing trouble seeing out of my right eye. I figured it was swelling shut. My cheek was also really hot for some reason. It had probably become swollen and cut from all the blows I had taken to the face. As the blurred double image of the samurai came toward me with Wakasashi in hand, I remember thinking to myself. *"Oh man...this is it, they're gonna gut me like a fish!"*

I couldn't' see crystal but I couldn't hear her either. Then again, with the ringing in my ears I could barely hear their annoying Asian babble let alone anything else.

Then, all of a sudden, that voice started screaming in my head again. *"You fucking idiot! Your legs! They don't have you legs pinned!"* It was so clear as if the person was right beside me talking to me. It was the only thing I could really hear over the ringing in my ears. But it was right, they didn't have my legs pinned down. These guys obviously didn't know what a kick boxer could do. As the Crimson Sword in front of me lifted the blade up to deal the death blow, I rolled forward quickly and drove my feet into his knees with all the strength I could muster. I watched his legs snap and fold in half backwards. As he was falling he swung his blade down, I rolled to the side and let it clang off the metal on my boots. It still put a gash in my calf, but it was still better than my stomach being cut open or worse yet, my head! While the two of them were stunned, I took the initiative; and, using the momentum from the roll, to axe kick down onto his wrist. Once again, I felt flesh and bone explode under the force and heard metal scream under the power of my kick. Then again, the scream could have been the samurai, considering I severed his wrist bone at the joint with that one. He quickly dropped the sword and I still had enough momentum to roll toward the other one and kick him square in the jewels! He cried out in agony, and I swear I felt something go POP!

Once his balance was gone, he was easy enough to Judo flip over my shoulder. By the time he hit the ground he found out how fast *I* was at drawing my Desert Eagle.
"Time to die bitch boy!" I snarled out as I

squeezed off about three shots in his head. Which pretty much made it disappear. My ears twitched, the sound of my Desert Eagle always seeming to clear them up. As I turned on my heel, ahead of me, the other samurai was already grabbing up his sword and getting to his feet. Even with his knees turned to scrap, this guy was quickly heading my way. *God damn it I can see how these guys got their reputation!"* But this time, I was ready! As he came just close enough, I leaped back doing a flip kick. It was like watching an action movie in slow motion; as my foot connected with his face I sent him backwards, shattering most of his teeth out of his mouth. As I spun around full circle in the air, I caught sight of a sign just above his air borne body. I leaned back and aimed carefully. I may not have been as fast as Crystal is on my feet, but I was the best damned shot around! I squeezed off about two rounds, both of which hit their mark: The wire holding a huge neon sign about a yard long. The sign screamed and groaned as the bullets ripped through its support wires. It shattered the thin piece of plasteel holding it up and came crashing down on top of the samurai's helpless body. "Mother fucker, I don't fucking care how god damn tough you are, I KNOW yer ass ain't gett'n up now!" I heaved and breathed a sigh of relief though my ribs were KILLING me! I blew the smoke off my barrel and spun it around a few times just to be a show off and put it back in its holster under

my coat.

"Now, back to Crystal." I said painfully, as I limped off back to the terminal beside the building. By about this time, Crystal was jacking out of the system. I could tell by the way her body shuddered like it was coming back to life. It was a sign that her consciousness had returned to her body. It was still creepy. Whenever she was fully disconnected from the system, she exclaimed as she looked me over.

"What the Hell happened to you!?"

"I had a little company I had to entertain." I said with a groan, as I pointed my thumb over my good shoulder. She looked at the headless Crimson Sword Samurai and the pile of rumble that was once a billboard then back to my bloody shoulder.

"Wow, you made quite a mess out here didn't you?" She smirked trying to hide her genuine concern for my well-being. As she moved closer to me I could have sworn she rubbed her boobs against me. The scary thing was, I think I liked it. She gently began to inspect my shoulder. She was being as careful as possible with it, but even the slightest movement caused me to cry out in pain and blood to squirt from the rather vicious wound.

"He really cut you deep. She said, further inspecting the wound. Almost all the tendons and the muscle are completely severed. The bone is pretty badly damaged too. We better get you to the hospital quickly!" I wanted nothing more than to just lay down. The pain was excruciating. But I knew what would happen if I left now. I would never get a decent run again in my life! I needed this run, and that meant I had to finish it no matter what.

...no..." I whispered weakly. I think I caught Crystal by surprise. She looked at me agape as she knelt down next to me.

"What did you say!?" She had a stunned expression her face. I would have been too being in her shoes. I looked up at her wincing at the pain.

"I said NO!" I almost shouted at her. "I need this job. If I quit now, I'll never get another one like it again. I'm not gonna quit now!" Crystal looked me in the eyes. I had never seen her so concerned.

"You do realize Raven, that if you don't' get this arm looked at immediately...you're chances of losing it to a prosthetic one are almost 100% right?" She seemed to be able to sense that I wasn't' much for prosthetics. "I don't care, I needed some upgrades anyway." I smirked weakly, trying to pretend like this wasn't as serious as it really was. Crystal reached into her tool belt and pulled out this small instrument that looked like an old mini vacuum that they used to use to clean keyboards out back in the early 21st centuary. I looked at it as she removed the sterile protector cap.

"The HELL is that!?" I asked, moving my arm away from her.

"It's an elastic-protein medical gel. It'll stop the hemorrhaging." She grinned at me as she shook the applicator lightly like a can of shaving cream in front of me.

"Can't have you passing out from loss of blood on me now can I Rave? Then I'd have to keep the payment for this job all for myself." She was pushing my buttons again. No more than like thirty seconds after finding out I'm alright she was talking about ripping me off again.

"You wish ya fucking slut! And DON'T fucking call me Rave, CRYSTAL!" I knew that irritated her. Just like calling me Rave burnt me up something awful. "And is this going to hurt?" I tried my best with the pain to make a come-back. Wasn't' a very good one though. She chuckled at me. "Oh yeah, A LOT!" Before I could get another word in edge-wise, she pushed the applicator into my wound and squeezed this awful smelling brown foam into my wound. Looked like shit mixed with shaving cream and smelt just about as bad!

I cried out in pain. *This is fucking torture!* It burnt like hellfire as soon as it touched the tender wound. She filled the gash till it overflowed the entry wound slightly, then covered it with a dry bandage.

"That should do it." She said as she took another

dry cloth and created a make-shift sling for my arm.

"I see someone passed their bio-tech coarse in High School." I kind of felt like a bitch for making a snide comment after she just doctored my arm. But I didn't know what else to say. I hadn't felt this cared for in a long time. I wasn't sure how to thank her for her kindness. She just smiled at my comment and simply replied.

"I learned a thing or two, that's all." She then looked over the building from where I was kneeling, it looked like she was trying to formulate a plan. I took my good old time standing up. I didn't want to stand up too fast and end up falling right back down. I looked over the building as well for a moment, then turned my attention back to Crystal.

"So, I said, assessing our current situation, what's the NEW plan?" She looked from me to the building then back to me again and said just simply.

"We'll go with Plan B of course. Simple enough." Yeah, the problem was, she never told me about a Plan B!

"PLAN B!?" I exclaimed, still wincing in pain, "The HELL did we come up with a Plan B?! How come you didn't tell ME about no Plan B?!" This was not the time for our communication to break down. She just laughed. "It's simple, she began, you cover me while I go in through the side and clear the hall ways. I blinked at her, I was expecting a punch line accompanied after that statement. When one didn't come, I shouted, "THAT'S your Plan B!? That's not much of a plan! Why don't' you just transfer the money from the terminal over there!?" She shook her head at me.

"Because I can't pull the money out of the system. They have it on a different terminal that's not connected to the main network." Most computer networks in the city of Seattle connect directly into the large internet set up we all call "The Network", or just "The NET" This makes a Decker's job usually very easy. But there are some terminals, like the one in this case, that don't connect in the Network.

This was definitely an odd case, however, considering most banks who deal with other people's money make the accounts readily available to all members of the community. Especially considering Brackhaven has over one million customers in the UCAS alone. Not to mention that it is also a global conglomerate, meaning that even in areas like Euro-Asia and the New Aztec Republic, you could get an account through Brackhaven. Providing you had the right financial backing that is. But I wasn't about to question Crystal on this. She was supposed to be the Decker here after all.

"Luckily though, I did manage to locate the terminal that the money is on. It's on the third floor." I wasn't' so sure about this whole Plan B thing. We were only two people here after all, and I had heard corp run stories where 5 and 6 runners were all gunned down and kept for corporate experiments after a botched corp run.

Urban myth maybe, but I really didn't feel like trying to debunk the myth tonight. Especially not in my condition.

"Do you really think this is gonna work? I asked looking over the building again. I mean, I got a gimp arm, and I know you're fast, but are you really THAT fast?" Crystal smiled at me.

"I have faith in you Raven. If you were able to stand up to two of those the Crimson Sword guys and come away with just a mangled shoulder, then you have real potential. Not just to be some two-bit criminal or meager low pay runner. I'm talking you have the potential to be more than just a runner. You could be a legend! I believe in your skills. I'm asking you to believe in mine as well. If you trust in me, trust in your partner then we can get through this! That I will promise you."

I couldn't argue with her anymore after a speech like that. That and I hurt too badly to think of something equally epic to say. Truth be told, I wanted nothing more than to prove myself and get back at the corps that destroyed my home. And this was a good way to start. If I couldn't handle this, then I had no hope of taking on a group like the one that I was told took out my home.

"...Then let's do this!" I said, with a sense of renewed vigor.

Drawing my Desert Eagle, I could tell I only had 10 shots left in the clip. I didn't need to look I could just FEEL the weight difference. It was a special talent I had picked up from working with guns so much. I slung the Ingram over my good shoulder and nodded to Crystal. This was it. We were about to cross the point of no return. This is where everything began. Right here, in this moment.

Chapter 3
The Shadows Call Pt. 3

July 2nd 2060 New Seattle
Downtown Neo-Seattle, Brackhaven Investment Firm
Main Building.

02:14:10AM.

"On the count of three; ready?" Crystal had her
hand on her sword and her boot ready to kick the
door open. I nodded as she began to count.
"One....
"THREE!" I shouted and kicked the door in and
dove forward. No sooner did the door fling open
and I dove than did gun fire break out. Several
armed Atlas Knight security officers were already
awaiting our entrance. Atlas Knight is the
personal mercenary group trained and paid by
Atlas Macro-technology. They had opened fire as
soon as the doors flew open. I thought I just lost
Crystal, I didn't think anyone was fast enough to
dodge out of the way of that one. As I landed I
rolled forward and was up on my knees firing at
the guards. A .50 cal. semi-auto packs a lot of
punch, even for Kevlar clad officers. But a Atlas
Knight's armor was different than your average
street legal crud. Sure it put them on their asses,
but it didn't keep them there!

"SHIT!" I cussed under my breath as I ducked
behind a partition, bullet fire ripping through the
plaster and cheaply masoned extension.
"They're wearing Riot gear! Gonna need all head

shots! Damnit Crystaleen!" I complained at her as a bullet zung by my face as I went to look around the wall, powdering me with plaster dust. "Why'd you pick now for me to move faster than you!?" But no sooner did I spit those words out and clear the dust from my eyes than I heard the sound of a blade pulling from its sheath. I poked my head from around the corner. The site in which I beheld was one of gruesome slaughter. And yet...enigmatic beauty. Crystal came rushing through the door and with amazing precision and accuracy, like she herself could SEE the very bullets as they were discharged from the barrels of officers' guns, she moved down the hall her blade ripped through their armor like a razor through silk.

She used their bodies like shields and spring boards, launching her supple form from one body to the next, slicing them to ribbons with quick skillful moves. I learned what the blue glow of the blade was, it was a magical blade that, when it struck, it sent waves of magical ice from its edge. She even used that as a weapon. Such beauty. I was awestruck. Even though I managed to pull myself together and follow behind her, I still did very little other than pick off a random guard breaking through the ice. I watched as she moved with lightning speed and reflex down the narrow hall. In combat, Crystal was a different person. So focused...so strong. She'd slice through one, spin around and thrust the blade through the back of the officer, then rebound, slice upward through the next, pivot on her heel, and slice the next through at the waist. She'd pirouette like a ballerina, as bullets flew past her; I could swear she could tell when they were going to fire, and slice straight through the guards.

Crystal carried two mini AK 97's that could be fired much like hand guns at her hips. But never once did she pull those guns. At the end of the hall, after rolling off another officer, she ran the final one through and froze him to wall and, with amazing speed and grace, sliced through him and three other frozen guards. There was a moment of silence; it was so nostalgic! I felt as though she had sliced through time and space itself. Her movements so quick and precise that, for that second, which felt like an eternity...time had to stop for just a millisecond to catch up with her. But in that time...I felt something...something familiar about her swordsmanship. As if..some time...a long time ago..I had seen it before. As soon as her blade clicked in place on her back everything, time, space, the blood at my feet and on my hands, began to move again. And the ice shattered leaving only bodies and chunks of ice behind. I could only stare at her. I was blushing I could feel it. I don't know if I was genuinely attracted to her or just so awestruck that I was at a loss for words. I do know that I managed these words.

"Th...that was frigg'n amazing!?!" I was having trouble swallowing the lump in my throat.

Up until now, I hadn't' realized just how tough Crystaleen Blue Blade really was! "Hmm?" She turned and looked at me. She didn't' have a scratch on her.

"OH! heh, yeah. I'm mostly a Street Samurai. I dabble in decking though. I take it you've never seen such swordsmanship? Or..perhaps by the look in your eyes..you have. You just can't remember it." She smiled at me. She could tell I was blushing. My face almost matched by burgundy hair.

"C'mon the elevator's just ahead!" She sprinted toward the elevator. I was still stunned then something hit me, like a voice again. It was screaming something about...*"LOOK AHEAD LOOK AHEAD!!!"* No sooner did I look up than I seen it! A remote gun drone popping up out of the floor. Now I don't' know much about drones themselves. But I could see from here that it was mounting a 65mm rapid cannon.

A weapon of that capacity could shred a light armor vehicle in 2.3 seconds; it would splatter a small Elvin body in a fraction of that. It felt like slow motion as I screamed to Crystal but there wasn't enough time! I did the only thing I could. I ran toward her. But she was already so far ahead of me! I'd never make it in time! That's when I saw it a piece of the partition on the wall that crystal had cut through was hanging loose. If I could hit it hard enough it would fall forward and I could get a clean shot at the drone. The only thing was it would require the use of my other hand and my Ingram. But my arm was useless and I'd need my right hand to fire my Desert Eagle! There was no way I could fire it from my left hand in the shape my left shoulder was in. "Only got one shot at this!" I said to myself as I yanked the strap of my Ingram down from my wounded shoulder. I almost stumbled over from the pain as I gripped it in my left hand and squeezed the trigger. The recoil was exasperatingly painful! The bullets ripped into weak partition and it came collapsing down.

I leaped up on it as it fell forward and ran about 3 steps then dove sideways in front of Crystal and fired my eagle. I squeezed off 9 shots to the words "You're.not.gonna.take.her.while.I'm.here.BITCH!" Each shot hit one of the barrels. By this time crystal had seen the drone and me dive in front of her. The shots caused the drone's shells to rupture prematurely, which cause it to blow upward and spin. As I landed, Crystal took one leap over me, drew her blade, and sliced through the drone like butter. As I skid on my bad arm on the dusty floor, she landed on her feet two foot from the elevator. Once again, as she sheathed her sword, the drone split in two and shattered into cubes of ice on the floor.
"How come I always get the painful landing?" I grumbled as I slowly pulled myself up on the wall groaning and covered in white plaster dust.
"Cause you're the newbie!" Crystal said coyly as she helped me up to my feet hitting the up button on the elevator. "Rule of the rookie. You take all the knocks!" She laughed. "C'mon let's go!" She said as she helped me into the elevator, the doors closing before us.

"Well, I coughed out, clearing plaster dust, gun smoke, and ash from my lungs, we got through the first floor."

"Yep, Crystal replied, pressing the third floor button. Now, as long as we don't' get stopped on the second floor and we don't' get killed on the third floor, we find the vault and we get the information and get out alive, we should be good." She smiled as if the job was easy.
"Hmm, horrible odds. I like it." Maybe I was woozy from the lack of blood, or maybe I was just cut out for this, but that was probably my first suicidal comment.
"I knew you had it in you. Nice shooting by the way. Ya probably saved my ass back there." She said as the annoying elevator music began to play. I grinned but tried to hide it. Didn't work well.
"Ah, it was nuttin. You'd have done the same for me."

"Yeah, but I can't shoot that well. That's the best shooting I've seen in a long time Raven." She smiled at me. I think I finally earned Crystal's respect.
"Any time Crystaleen." I gave her a thumbs up about all I could do, my arm was hurting so bad.
"That sword swinging wasn't too shabby either. Aint too many people who can slice through a titanium armored mini assault drone and a hallway full of Atlas Knights and walk away unscathed."

"You can call me Crystal, Rave. Yeah, I got some skill. Your arm still hurting you?" She said noticing my heavy breathing. I nodded.

"Yeah, I grimaced, I think I severed the bone between firing the sub-machine gun and landing on it back there. And yet again I threw up. By now, I had nothing left in my stomach. "Well that feels a bit better. Now that I have nothing left in my stomach to make me wanna throw up. Heh...oWw!" Genuinely I wasn't doing so hot now.

"Hang on." She said, as she began digging through her munitions belt. She pulled out what looked like an oversized band-aid. I looked at it and arched a brow.

"Hey Crystal, I appreciate the thought and all, but I don't' think a really big band-aid is gunna do much for this one, despite the commercials."

"Just hold still a moment!" She applied it to my arm. There was a sharp burning feeling then the pain dulled away and I felt a lot better.

"Hell I feel like a million credits now! What was that?" She chuckled as the elevator dinged at the third floor.

"Stim-patch. Used to numb pain, stop some minor bleeding and gives you an adrenal boost so long as you wear the patch. It'll last 24 hours from the time of application. By no means a fix-all, but it should get you through the rest of this mission." I smiled and nodded as I reloaded my Desert Eagle and cocked the chamber back.

"Let's do it!"

As the elevator dinged and the doors slid open the elevator was thrashed with a hail of automatic gun fire. The guards on the third floor shot the elevator full of holes, not wanting to wait for us to step out, knowing full well what we did to the guards on the first floor. They riddled the

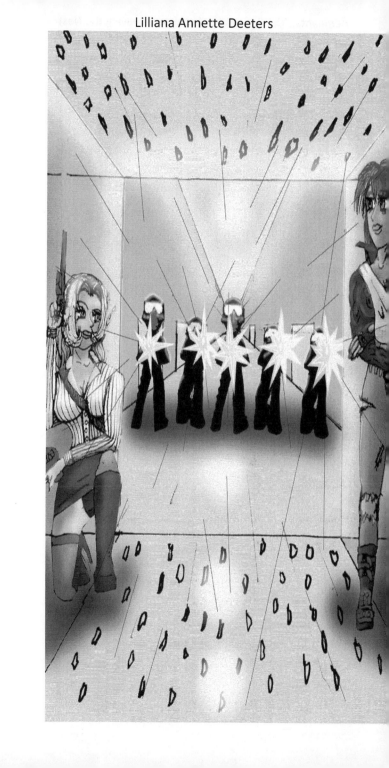

beautiful tiled floor and cheery wood finished walls full of holes. When the onslaught of bullets was finished it was thought impossible for ANYTHING to have survived. The finished tile floor was a dusty shattered mess. It looked more like cheese than a floor. The once beautiful Cherry wood walls were shredded and falling in on the now Swiss-cheese looking floor. Only the black powder burnt brushed steel remained in its stead.

"They always have to shoot the elevator when it first opens." Crystal whispered to me as the hail of bullets continued bombard the small chamber. She was safely hidden along the side of the elevator where the buttons for floors was. Knowing that that section was hidden behind about 10 feet of plastcrete and steel. I was on the directly opposite side of her, which was also safely positioned between the same mass of masonry.

"Don't' they ever watch the old Net clips? Ya never fire till the people show themselves. Oh well." I smirked as I waited for the sound of automatic weapons running out of ammo. I knew they'd have to reload eventually. And sure enough, soon we heard the clicking sound of SMG's and Assault rifles going dry.

"Cross ways? "Crystal looked at me with the same shit-eating smirk as mine.

"Yep! Automatic weapon fire." I replied and ran diagonally out of the elevator and pointed my Ingram toward the guards, opening fire as I ran.

Crystal wasn't far behind as she darted out across my line of fire, timing her exit so that she would start firing just as I stopped and pass by me between bursts. She was damn good! We ran down the hall way, dodging behind pillars as we ran. Each time our weapons ran dry we reloaded and switched sides of the floor. Crossing each other's line of fire each time. I think she nicked my ear once. I knew it was bleeding when we were done. I think I nicked her cheek though cause I know it was bleeding too but that's beside the point! By the time we were all done I had half a clip left in my Ingram. Crystal was putting two new clips in her SMG's.

"Nice moves." I said as I strung my Ingram over my shoulder again. Now I really liked this girl! She could shoot ALMOST as well as me.

"Thanks. That means a lot coming from a gun-slinger like you." She replied sincerely. So I had to say something all sage-like or I'd not feel like myself.

"Though your aim could use a lil work. I think you nicked my ear. It's bleeding." I figured I'd just play ignorant to the fact that I think I got her cheek. She smiled taking the clips and a set of keys from the guards tossing me a couple clips. "Well, maybe you could teach me?" She said as she smiled all flirtatious over her shoulder at me. I blushed of course. She really was kind of irresistible.

"S-sure." I replied clearing the squeak from my throat. "Maybe you can teach me some new moves with that sword of yours." For some reason that sounded like I was coming onto her in so many ways and even my shit ass grin made it look like it. I remember thinking that I was a little gay in the back of my head.

She grinned with an accomplished smile, I figured she took it as a flirt as well. Which was bad on my part! "Sure thing Rave. Let's move!" "Yeah...lets!" I wanted to end that conversation before I really stuck my boot in my mouth!
"So, I said, inspecting the hallway. Do we have any clue which room the main frame is in?" The hallway, though now riddled with bullet holes and dead bodies, was long and actually rather spacious for what I thought corp
hallways would look like. It was also ornately decorated with decorative pillars which were now filled with bullet holes as well. One of the many rooms, to either side of this hall that we were standing in, were offices that the keys from the guard we killed went to. The problem was, Crystal, if she knew, hadn't told me which door the main computer was behind. Though ransacking a corp office was always fun and ideal, we had already made a lot of noise. We needed to hurry and get out of here. Crystal might have disabled the alarms for now, but I had a feeling the corp deckers were on the case as we roamed these halls.
"I'm not a hundred percent on that." She said as she looked through the small rectangular windows on the office doors, trying to see inside the offices looking for a main computer. "The info I got from the outside terminal didn't' really give me a specific office. It just said third floor. It aint the best deck in the world. Nor are they the best

progs in the world either. My cut of this mission is going to new deck, softs and if I got enough, some hards as well."

She said as we moved from office to office. I wasn't a genius when it came to decking, but I could gather that softs meant decking programs used to make a deck more powerful. And hards were like the deck itself and/or the memory slots inside for storage which most deckers called mem. We got about halfway down the second hall when I saw the lights flicker and I heard the hum of electrical equipment kicking back on. "Tell me dats not what I think it is!" I said as I stopped dead in my tracks in the hall. Crystal looked about the hallway real quick then ducked around a corner.

"Shit!" She cussed as she looked up at the camera begin rotating on the wall. "They must have gotten the security system up and running again. This is bad! If those cameras spot us the alarms will go off. I looked at her like she was an imbecile.

"No fucking shit Crystal! I'm not THAT frigg'n green now!" I peeked around the corner at the camera cussing under my breath.

"This is taking too long!" Crystal started slowly sneaking down the hall. She made it under the camera just as it was getting ready to swing back her way. I made sure I was out of site when it scanned down my way. As it began to swing back toward the other end of the hall, Crystal motioned to me to start down the hall.

I'm not too good at being patient, calm, delicate, or very kind. Needless to say I got spotted but it wasn't' enough to really set off the alarm. But I did hear someone in the near-by security office starting to move.

"Oh fuck alotta dis shit!" I said as I ran over to the office door way. Crystal went pale when she seen me.

"Rave what in the fucking hell do you think you're doing?!" She yelled my way, trying not to let her voice go above a loud whisper. Though she was obviously concerned but unable to move as the camera was just now starting to swing back her way. She was about to risk running across the hall to snatch me up when I kicked the security office door in right on the corp decker's face. He tumbled over himself not knowing what exactly hit him. He no sooner stood up about to ask me who the hell I was when I blew his ass away with my Desert Eagle. I shot him about three times that was pretty much the extent of it for him. Once he was out of the way, I waved to Crystal who looked down the hall then back up again real quick and ran across the hall. I was all smiles when she got over to me until she slugged me in the face. The bitch could hit too! I wasn't quite sure WHAT hit me at that point and swung around and just about clocked her till I realized what happened. I screamed at her.

"The frigg'n hell did you frigg'n hit me for ya fucking crazy ass bitch!?" I think I was actually more hurt than upset.

"Are you insane!? She yelled at me as the throbbing in my cheek began to grow. You could have gotten yourself KILLED! Its one thing to be brash in the heat of combat, but doing shit like that all the time during a run will get you and yer group killed! This is why I don't' work with amateurs! They think they can go all gun-ho on people and no one will catch them. This isn't' a game! Nor is this fucking action sim Raven! This is REAL FUCK'N LIFE! You EVER do some stupid ass thing like that again and you'll be pick'n yerself up off the ground!" At that point, she stormed away from me and started working on the mainframe which, was conveniently, in this room. Jacking into the system just as she did before. I watched her shudder and go all zombie-like.

Well, let's just say I was dumb founded now as well as hurt. I really did like Crystal. Maybe more than I thought was normal but I liked her. I also looked up to her even though I really didn't show it much. I felt like...like I let her down. To me, that was worse than honestly getting killed or hit by her.

I didn't really say anything to her after that. Even after she jacked out and we got the money transferred I stayed quiet. We escaped the building using a fire exit. I stayed quiet. She didn't' really say anything to me either. I thought; "*Well, this is it. Ya dun fragged it all up now Raven. Ya just had to be a show off.*" I thought to myself. I wanted to cry. But this wasn't the time. There'd be plenty of time for that back home. "...I'm gonna be stuck baby sitt'n corp lemmings fer da rest of mai life....." I said quietly under my breath as we arrived at the alley where Crystal's car was parked. Crystal's one ear twitched as she raised her brows and looked down at me. She heard me.

"Hmmm? Baby-sitting? Da hell would ya wanna do that kinda boring job fer? I know the corp run wasn't the best but it wasn't a complete nightmare either. We both made it out with our limbs. Well, yers is all fragged up but it's still there." She said making light of my arm situation.

I looked up at her. I was actually surprised she heard me so I was a little confused at first.
"Huh!? Oh! You heard me did ya?" I said then looked back down, holding my thrashed arm. She smirked,
"Yeah, my ears do more than frame my pretty face as well. What's wrong? Can't handle the corp run thing? They don't always turn out like that ya know?" I shook my head and looked up slightly.
"Nah it aint dat. I just assumed dat you didn't want me as yer partner no more considering you said I was too gun-ho." She blinked at me a moment, then she broke out in laughter. I was almost offended...ALMOST.
She laughed loudly,
"Hunneh, if all veteran runners refused to work with novice runners who were "gun-ho" at first, then I wouldn't be a runner either. Hell their wouldn't' be any NEW runners at all then." I looked up at her. I felt like a damn little kid! But

yet at the same time, she was the only one who
had taken the time to help me so far...
"So, ya still want me as yer partner?" I asked as I
looked up at her trying NOT to sound like a damn
rookie. It wasn't working well.

She smiled at me and ran her fingers through
my hair. Between being upset, hurt, and just all
around enamored by her skill, it caused me to
shudder and stumble into her. Boy was I
embarrassed! I'd never had feelings like that
toward a woman before. Hell, I used to think
homosexuals of any kind was whacked and
creepy. But there I was, my faced buried in a nice
set of soft warm breasts, my battered ass, thrashed
arm useless, a soft, gentle hand on my head
stroking my hair softly, a warm heart beat on my
hot sore cheek and a gentle caress across the tired
sore muscles of my back. I knew then I was
definitely the same color as my hair. But for
some reason, I didn't care. I hadn't felt this close
to someone in years. It was nice to be special
again. Even if in a city of hate, deceit, pain,
suffering, coldness, darkness, bleak, black,
hypocrisy and sadness....we were nothing more
than two specs embracing in the dim street lights.
"...it's alright Raven. I'm here for you. And I'm
not gonna leave you go any time soon. Let's go
home."

Chapter 4
Guns, Cars, and Girls

July 16th 2060 New Seattle

I spent the next two weeks in the hospital. They had to replace my arm with a cyber-arm. It took almost all our cut from the run to get a new arm and make it look somewhat human like. I remember Crystal telling me that having obvious cyber ware makes the STAR more suspicious of you. So I had to get a replacement that looked somewhat human. This is also known as Prosthetics body parts. It's a growing fad amongst high end gang members and more experienced runners. And I say "high end", because it's an expensive surgery. Needless to say, it may look human, but the person who has the part knows better. I remember them putting me under but that's about it. The Doc said the surgery went well. But when I woke up, it felt like it went bad. And I couldn't figure out why my other arm hurt so much. When I awoke, I saw Crystal asleep by my side. My arm was stiff and hard to stretch at first. Which is what I usually do first thing in the morning. Once I got the hang of moving it around, I reached out and touched her head. She stirred and groaned, mumbled something about it being too early. I had no

frag'n clue what time it was. I just woke up.
"Crystal." I whispered softly. I don't know why I
always chose to whisper in hospitals. Something
from my past just told me to do it. She whined
and grumbled again and yawned looking up at me.
Her make-up was a wreck and so was her hair.
She had changed clothes but it looked like she
hadn't really cleaned up properly during my entire
stay here.

"Oh...you're awake?" She said tiredly as she
stretched and scratched her head, trying to fix her
mangled do. Her hair was all over the place. It
looked like someone zapped her with a tazer gun.
I couldn't help but laugh. But even that hurt right
now. I chuckled then grimaced at her.
"Yep, it'll take more than that to keep me down."
I smiled weakly. She smiled and stretched again.
"How's yer arm feel Rave? It looks like you've
regained use of it." She asked, with a softness in
her voice I still wasn't quite accustomed to.
"Yeah its fine. My other arm is the one that hurts
though for some odd reason." I complained as I
rubbed my still flesh and blood arm. She fixed
her hair some-what and smiled. "It's probably the
new nervous system the doc installed. He said it
may take some gett'n used to." I looked up at her
at that point then around at room. It wasn't a very
spectacular room. We were at the "Body Mall."
It's an old joint just inside downtown Redmond.
Cheapest place to get cyber ware in all of
Redmond.

Probably in all of Seattle. They do some prosthetic work but mostly with limbs. I was glad it was my arm not anything else like an eye or an ear. The room was shaudy and bleak at best. Done in a dingy gray color. The sheets still had blood stains on from the last "patient". The walls looked like they could use about three new coats of paint and the windows were barred off. The spectacular view I had, was that of a side of another brick building. Tre-chic right? Not really. The accommodations for guests weren't very good either. The chair that Crystal had to sit on was an old folding steel chair. And even it wasn't in good condition.

"Did you stay with me the entire time?" I asked. I half expected to wake up with a note saying *"Nice run kid, here's your cut, hope you can afford to pay for year arm with this."* But instead, I awoke to find a beautiful but rather haggard young woman at my bed side. I wasn't used to that. As far as I knew, my whole life I had been alone. After I asked Crystal this, she got silent and I could tell she was blushing. It was a very awkward moment of silence. After about 2 minutes, which seemed like an hour, she answered me.

"I figured it would be nice to have someone to wake up to." She said it so plainly that I should have known it the whole time. But yet I still couldn't grasp the reality of what she was saying. I just stared at her for a moment. She continued from that point.

"When I first got my data jack and my other

various cyber-ware installed, I had no one to wake up to. Waking up in a hospital alone is a lonely, empty feeling. No one should have to feel lonely and empty inside." I had no clue the gravity that Crystaleen's words would have on me in the near future. Or the striking effect she still has on me to this day. But even then, I felt for the first time...in a long time, like I finally had a real friend. I smiled up at her with tears in my eyes and simply said.

"Thanks a lot...sister."

August 6th, 2060 New Seattle
Redmond Barrens District, Raven's Apartment
12:30:12pm

It took three weeks of therapy for me to learn to fully use my right arm again without having any problems making natural movements with it. By this time, we were hard up for cash for this month's rent. Being unable to do a run for three weeks kind of puts one at a loss for cash! We had to come up with something. Luckily, I had a little gun repair shop on the side that I ran outside of my home. It was a good way to make quick cash. That and I loved taking guns apart and tinkering with them anyway. Crystal told me she was going to move in with me. When I asked her why she told me that it was because she'd never make enough money to make her rent this month so she was just going to split rent with me. That would be a lot simpler than just me having to pay my rent. Rent for my pad was 5000 credits. Cheaper than hers which was closer to 50,000!

When I arrived home I had to have like, fifty messages on my machine. And they were all from the same annoying little dwarf Chip. Apparently he had heard about me being in the hospital and that I had spent all my share of the run on my new cyber arm. So he had been trying to get a hold of me. Most likely to make sure I didn't' bleed his name out to anyone or anything like that. People in this city don't' really care about you. Just the information you have. I rolled my eyes and decided to sign on and dialed his digits. The phone rang for a bit then picked up but there was no video. I heard chips voice on the other side.

"...Hello?" He seemed unsure of who was on the other end of the line.

"Chip, the hell are you doing? Turn yer damn vid on!" I yelled to him.

"Who's this?" He asked, as if he didn't' recognize my voice.

"You frag'n half pint moron! Its ME, Raven! Turn on yer damn vid!" I shouted at him, getting rather agitated at the fact that I was being treated like a suspect in a murder trial. Finally, he turned on his video feed and tried to cover up the fact that he was all paranoid with his big dorky dwarven smile.

"Oh! Raven! HI! Wassup? I didn't' think it was you. Sorry about that! Soooo...how's the arm? He said with a less-than-convincing grin. I just glared at him.

"....yeah...right...not convincing! I didn't tell anyone anything about you or yer damn "side jobs"! And yer lying skills need some work there! I suggest you stick to being a fixer! And I need a favor from you." Chip thought about it a moment then answered.

"Umm, why should I do you a favor? And I'm guessing this is supposed to be a free favor?" I grumbled at him.

"You dumb ass hole! I just did a run for you and got my arm all thrashed to hell and back and you can't do me a favor?" I was still sore so I wasn't' really in a good mood. He blinked at me and grinned again.

"But I paid you for that job Raven." He grinned all accomplished like. Chip wasn't' very good of a liar. But he was a damn good business negotiator. I groaned. I had a feeling I was going to have to pay for this.

"Sooo, Raven, how much can I do you for?" Just about then, Crystal sat down and started talking. "Yo Chip this is Crystal!" His face dropped.

"Oh, hello Crystal. I didn't know you were there. Is there something the matter?" I just blinked. I had a feeling this wasn't going to go well.

"Yeah there is actually Chip. Ya see, this my new place. Yeah, I'm moving in with Raven here and we need to make rent this month. So, why don't you go round up some peeps who need their weapons customized and I'll try to forget that STAR officer's phone number!" She glared at Chip with a look that I hadn't' seen her use before. If I didn't know better, I'd have thought she was serious. Chip was completely silent for a moment. Then, after about two minutes, he finally spoke up.

"Alright, I got this girl, she's kinda green like Raven, but she's good! She's a tinkerer. She can do a lot of work with you girls' vehicles. I'll send her your way so Raven can fix up her weapons. Okay!?" I was stunned at how quickly Chip lost control of the conversation.

Crystal smirked with an accomplished look on her face. "That's what I thought, thanks for yer time Chip!" Chip snorted and signed off without another word. Crystal turned to me and just smiled with a sage-like nod; then stood and made her way to the bathroom.

"Well, I'm gonna take a shower Rave. Have fun!" She began her sashay toward the bathroom when I spoke up. "Wow, Crystal. If I didn't' know better, I'd have believed you really WERE approached by a STAR officer!" She just smiled over her shoulder as she pulled her top off she had no bra on underneath it and looked back at me. "I was approached by one while you were out getting your arm worked on." She raised her brow and smirked. "But I'm not a traitor. I wouldn't' do that to you. I have honor. She stepped into the bathroom and closed the door. I was just stunned. I sat there quiet till my cigarette burned out. ...."Seriously!? What the fuck!?"

August 13th 2060, New Seattle
Redmond Barrens District. Raven's Apartment
14:01:00pm

    About one week after Crystal and Chip had their little "talk" I got a knock at my door. At the time I was in my bra and a pair of pants with just my leather hanging off my shoulders. I had a beer in one hand and smoke hanging off my lip. I looked at the door, then up to Crystal.
"I'm not expecting anyone. Are you?" I asked her, with a look of concern on my face. Crystal moved her gaze from me

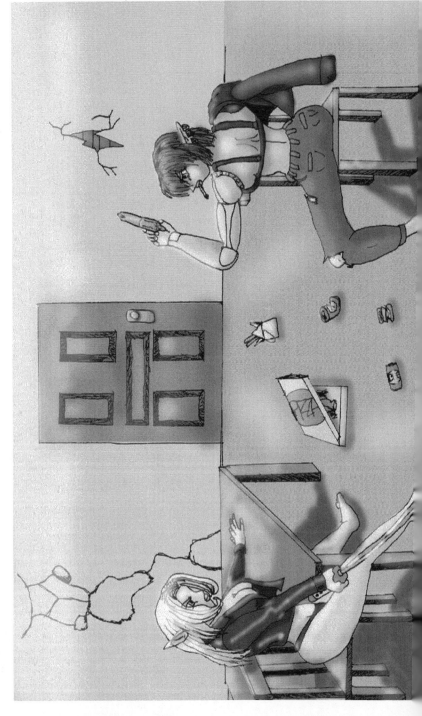

to the door, she had her jacket on with no shirt or bra underneath and was just in her panties. "Neither am I." She replied. I had been working on my specialized ammunition. My hyper velocity Armor Piercing ammo. Most HV ammo is fired at an accelerated rate of speed by adding extra powder to the shell casing. But, weapons that fire that kind of ammo have to be reinforced or else the powder flash and rapid bursts chew up the inside of your barrel real fast. It's an expensive process for ammo that actually only flies at a medium to close range to get the full piercing effect.

And Armor Piercing Ammo uses specialized solid slugs that are fired from the shell case. When they hit, instead of mushrooming like hallow points, shredding apart like Flecthett Head shells, or just flattening out like a normal bullet. They actually punch a whole straight through. I'm sure you all have heard of "Cop Killers". These bullets have tephlon coated projectiles which blow through Kevlar and other such light armor. There's also full metal jacket rounds which pierce tough armor. These are all AP ammunition. Now, the problem with AP ammo is first of all its expensive as hell to buy! Second, they don't just sell the frag'n shit on every street corner. And most importantly, the shit is heavy as all hell to carry around. Plus it has a really bad habit of setting off alarms. So, I got the bright idea of combining to the two types of ammo into one. You got the HV which will move really fast and is really light weight. Plus, you got the punching power of AP that can be fired at a longer range and still keep the same effect. Not to mention I use a modified Desert Eagle soo...yeah you get the idea.

Well, since there's no such thing as this type of ammo on the market. And apparently no one was intelligent enough to figure out how to make it. I decided I'd put it together myself. Biggest problem is the components. I narrowed it down to five main components. First, is the shell casing. I can't be using conventional casing cause it won't withstand the blast of the powder. And if I use really heavy metal, it'll just weigh me down. So, I figured that an alloy metal, like titanium or such would be best. Light weight but strong as shit! Second, the combustible! I figured I couldn't go with conventional flash or bang powder. (That's black powder or gun powder for you laymen out there). So, I figured I'm going to have to go with a more chemical combustible. Now, problem with this is, if I go with too big a boom, I'll blow the gun apart and probably most of my arm along with it. So, stuff like Nitro and that is not a wise choice. BUT, if I use a more condensed oxygen blast, I should be able to power the shell at a higher velocity than just using conventional gun powder. I know, it sounds all complex but it's really quite simple. You make an oxygen pocket in the shell that is suddenly exposed to a fire spark. IE, the spark from when the hammer hits the bullet's casing. Thus, creating a sudden blast much like the way a car engine fires a piston to propel a car.

Also similar to a Gauss rifle, minus the whole magnet thing. Third, the reinforcement for my gun so it doesn't blow the frag apart! Now, I know I said in the last step that I didn't want to use a combustible that would blow my gun and my arm off. But friends, no matter what you do new to a gun, you must always, ALWAYS add reinforcements where necessary. I've broken it down into three main areas I need to adjust my gun. First; chamber, duh! When this bullet is loaded its going be a different size than a normal shell. So, I have to adjust the size of the chamber. This is going be the hardest part cause if I'm off by even a fraction of a millimeter, the gun could explode in my face! You see, when a shell loads into a chamber of a gun, if the chamber is not properly oiled and/or cleaned. The shell can stick or load crooked. Causing a jam. Or, a really bad back fire. Trust me friends, I've seen some BAD back fires. Ever wonder what a human head would look like without the skin attached? I'll have to show you the file some time.

Anyway! So yeah, I need to file down or expand out the chamber. Second would be the barrel itself. If you have a gun at home my fellow runners, and I'm sure you do, take a look down the barrel of it once. And try not to blow your frag'n brains out while doing it! I suggest you unload it first. And make sure there isn't a bullet in the chamber. But, as you look down the barrel, (sometimes it helps to hold it up to a light in your loft), you'll see that it has what look like threads inside it. These threads are what the bullet follows so that it doesn't hit the side of your barrel and explode in your face. Yes again. A gun is a very delicate piece of machinery. If the barrel's not cleaned and properly oiled it can blow your ass apart just as easily as the bullet. But anyway, these threads, known as rifling, will have to be adjusted so that the new shells can fire from the gun without any jamming or vibration.

And third the firing mechanism. AKA, the hammer or firing pin. A normal Desert Eagle firing pin is comprised of a hardened metal alloy which is different for each model. Most common is a steel/graphite mixture. Mine's a little...harder than that. But then I don't think I should say much more. None of my weapons are exactly legal per-say. But I will have to reinforce it some more. If you don't reinforce your firing pin guess what will happen? That's right! You guessed it friends! It'll blow up in your face yet again! When the hammer strikes the shell it causes a spark which ignites the gunpowder which then explodes and propels the shell forward out of the gun. The flash from the powder; IE the "back blast" fires from around the hammer usually in automatics. At least what doesn't come out the barrel does. In revolvers it fires from around the cylinder but that's another subject entirely. Back on subject, I will need to reinforce the hammer so that it can handle the stress from the more intense back blast coming from the new combustible. Once I fix these three things on my piece, it should be able to fire the new ammo without any problem. Which all this leads into the next piece of equipment I'll need. Fourth most, the projectile heads.

A HV bullet and AP bullet projectile head we covered earlier. Since these two types of bullets serve, for the most part, the same basic purpose. But do not necessarily have the same basic components. It is only logical to theorize that, for instance, a HV bullet should be able to equip the same heavy projectile head that an AP round does but, with a faster combustible, achieve the equivalent distance as a normal AP round would. Thus, creating a more effective munitions round with optimal stopping power. I've decided that the best type of head would be some of Atlas MacroTech's new hyper dense, hyper light weight metals that they're experimenting with for their newest Atlas Knight recruits. And the fifth and final piece of equipment I'm going to need is the proper tools and chemistry equipment to put it all together. What I wouldn't give for a frag'n modern day alchemist. Would make this SOO much easier! But that's just a fairy tale. No such thing as alchemy. At least not these days. This is probably going be one of the hardest things to acquire. Another item they don't' just sell on a normal street corner. Getting this will require a lot of careful planning. But since I don't have jack diddly squat right now, I'm going to quit boring you all with my rambling and get back to what's happening right now.

Crystal and I both moved in stereo. I took the right side of the door, so whoever was on the other side would be seeing me on their left and Crystal to their right. Opposite me. We slowly turned the handle of the door and left it slowly creep open. We waited till we heard at weak "....umm..hello?" Then we made our move. I rolled around the corner and pointed my Desert Eagle into a young girl's face. Crystal made the corner a split second after me with her blade at the girls' throat.
"FREEZE FRAG FACE!" I screamed at her, jamming the barrel of my gun into her forehead. "Keep yer hands where I can see'm or I'll blow yer frag'n brains out the back of yer gaw damn head!" The poor girl was so scared, I was surprised she didn't wet herself. She was a simple girl. Dressed in a camo halter and old greasy long johns. She had a dingy red handkerchief in her pocket and a wrench in the other. The name "Charlie" was on the upper right part of her long johns and on the upper left was the name "Lefties Garage". Her face, which had a look of utter terror on it now, was smudged with dirt and her hair was short, razor cut and looked like it could

use a washing. She had a big pair of glasses on that rested at the end of her nose. No make-up and her left hand was obvious cheap cyber junk. Must be where the name "Lefties Garage" came from. She threw her hands up and flailed them around wildly. Yelping and squealing like a complete imbecile.

"Oh please no no no no no! Don't shoot me don't shoot me! I didn't' do it! I was told to come here by a guy name Chip! He said a woman named Raven would fix my gun for me if I fixed her car! Please don't kill me! I'm too young to die!" Her eyes were huge and she had sweat pouring down her face. A little green like me? Damn, this girl was so green she'd be invisible in a forest! I looked out around her to see if anyone was with her. I didn't' see anyone so I asked her. " You alone girl?!" I asked as I glared into her eyes. She just squeaked.
"Umm....??" She was so frightened she didn't' know what to say. So I repeated myself a little more "clearly" this time.
"I SAID are you ALONE YOU LIL TWIT!?? I gotta blow that grime out from between ya ears for ya grease monkey!?" I clicked the hammer back on my Desert Eagle. I was bluffing of course, but I figured if she was really new at this, she'd crumple like a paper cup. I was right. A little more right than I wanted to be sadly. The poor little tinker girl dropped to her knees holding her head and started crying. Quite annoyingly I

might add! "WWWAAAHHHHAAAA!!!!!... "
She squalled louder than a cat in heat.
" Oh please oh please oh please don't kills me! I
was told to come here! PLEASE!!
WAAAAAAAHHH!!! I promise I'll run away
really fast if you just don't kill me!" She
continued to ball like scared baby. I just kind of
blinked down at her as she begged for her life at
my feet. I was starting to kind of feel really bad
for going that far.

"Umm...hey..I was just kidding ya know? I
was just gonna kinda hurt ya a bit. I wasn't really
gonna kill ya..." I wasn't quite sure how to handle
this one. I no sooner got that out of my mouth
than she started crying louder. I got all worried
and uncomfortable. Crystal helped her up and
looked at me and whispered in my ear.
"I think you came on a little strong there Raven.
Very nice though! Maybe ya shoulda quit at the
"Are you alone" comment." She nodded Sagely
again while she whispered to me and helped the
young girl inside. I moved out of the way and
shut the door scratching the back of my head with
the tip of my gun barrel.
"Really? I asked all dumb founded. I thought it
was pretty good too! But I didn't' know she was
gonna break down and cry and almost wet herself
on our door step?!" I shrugged and locked the
door. Crystal got her calmed down enough so
she'd stop cater wailing and got her a drink of tea.
Yes, she wanted tea! Once she got her bearings
back she told us who she was.
"Hello..my name's Charlie. Chip told me about
you two. I'm a tinkerer. I specialize in

modernizing cars and getting them road worthy
and the newest features. I lost my left hand when
a big corp tried to take over my garage. I
wouldn't let them buy me out so they arranged
an.."accident" where I lost my left hand. I'm a left
handed mechanic you see. Without my left hand,
I couldn't work. And it took all my funds to buy a
replacement hand. Now I make what money I can
by tricking out cars for runners like you guys. I'm
looking for work. And some help with my gun.
If you need anything vehicle related...I'm yer
girl!" I felt a connection with this girl. I felt like
her story was similar to mine some-how. Though
I didn't' even know my OWN story. I did know
one thing though. The mega corps had made her a
pawn in their war for power. And as far as I was
concerned; that made her an ally in my book!

August 27th 2060 New Seattle

Redmond Barrens District, Raven's Apartment
19:15:11pm

It took approximately two weeks to get
Charlie's gun up to standards. Well, MY
standards anyway. Which are apparently higher
than Atlas' standards. The original revolver she
had, which was a simple .38, was bought almost
directly from an Atlas dealer. It was actually a

gift from her father before he passed away. From what Charlie told me, her father had it for a long time and kept up with the maintenance. I will admit, it was in pretty frigg'n good condition for being an older model. But the cylinder's capacity was shit and you had to pull back the hammer then pull the trigger. Not exactly a very effective strategy in a world filled with semi and full auto weapons you know? So I increased her ammo capacity to 9, instead of 6, and made it so she could just pull the trigger rather than have to pull the hammer back. I will admit, revolvers jam less than automatics, but automatics reload faster. Depends what you like I guess.

After I had her gun up to standards, I went about discussing "payment" for my services. It was getting close to the end of the month and my landlord had already been breathing down my frigging neck for a week!

"Alright Charlie, I said putting my tools away and cleaning up my work bench, you got what you needed. Now let's talk about what WE need. Ya see, I'm back on my rent and my car could use a lil work. So, since I got you all fixed up, how about returning the favor? Plus I could use a couple creds to make rent this month." Crystal grinned from the kitchen where she was preparing some soy caf for the three of us.

"Oh, Charlie said to me, as if she was totally surprised, I don't have any money either Raven." She said it like she was so innocent! It was quite annoying actually!

"WHAT!?" Came at the same time from both myself and Crystal in the kitchen. "What do ya mean ya ain't got no money!? The frag'n hell did you expect to PAY for the gun!?" I so wanted to kill her right there and then. But I could feel Crystal's eyes on the back of my head. Urging me to hear her side of the story. So I waited. Charlie shrank back into her chair, her eyes getting really huge again like the first time we met at the door.

 "Ummm...ch..Chip told me I was just supposed to fix up yer cars for you. He didn't say I had to pay for the gun. He said you'd trade for it. I..I swear I didn't know! Please don't hurt me!!" It was obvious by the way she was flailing her arms about aimlessly that she was telling the truth. "Damn you Chip you sneaky bastard!" I sighed as I slouched back in my dusty old chair rubbing the bridge of my nose. This whole thing was starting to give me a headache. I looked up at Crystal as she came out of the kitchen with the soy caf for the three of us. Assuring Charlie that I wasn't going to kill her, this time.

"So, I said to Crystal, what are we gonna do now?" Hoping she'd have an answer. She looked to me sadly with a defeated look upon her face as she placed the small cups in front of us.
"I'm sorry Raven but, Chip was as much my fixer as he was yours. Obviously he's flown the coop by now. Thinking that we're gonna squeal to the STAR. I'm afraid I'm outta ideas. We could try to find a Johnson at one of the local pubs but it could take weeks to build up enough creds to make rent doing that." I sighed and shook my head. "We don't have that much time. Damnit! now were'

screwed!" I thought this was just great! I survived a corp run and an attack by the Crimson Sword for this? Not the way I had envisioned going out. Getting tossed out onto the street because I couldn't make rent. After a moment or two, Charlie spoke up on her own.

"Umm..I might have an idea." She said, after getting our attention by clearing her throat.

"Really? I asked. YOU have an idea?" At first I looked at Crystal. Unsure if I should trust this girl. However, Crystal just shrugged. I guess she was thinking the same thing I was. What the hell do we have to lose right? Charlie nodded as she took a sip from her cup.

"Yeah it's not much but how about I go over it with you after I take a look at yer cars?" She asked warming up to us a little bit more. "Sure! I said feeling not so defeated now. It's gotta be better than sitting here waiting for my eviction notice."

"Great! She chirped, finishing her cup of soy caf and placing the cup down on the table in front of her. Just show me to yer garage!" We walked Charlie out to the back of my apartment.

"Garage? What frig'n garage?" Was all I could say. She walked around our cars she looked the vehicles up and down very sage-like. She rattled off the exact make and model of Crystal's Viper and the exact make and model of my cheap ass beater. She walked all around them, opened the doors, trunks, hoods, dove, head first, under the hood of each car and rattled off more car pieces, parts, models and things that sounded totally

Greek to the both of us.

I understood at that point what it must be like for people when I started talking about my guns. "Alright!" She suddenly just chimed out, poking her head out from under the hood of my car, her face was all covered with soot and was smeared with grease. She reminded me a bit of a football player. With the black paint they wear under their eyes and across their nose. "I can fix these up to standard."
"Up to standard!?" Crystal exclaimed. I really didn't have much to say about my POS. "My Viper is top-of-the line! I've never missed an oil change nor a rotation of the tires. How can it be NOT up to standards?" Charlie wriggled her little body out from under the hood of Crystal's car. Even her Tee and over-alls were covered with soot and grease. She wiped her hands and part of her face off on the handkerchief she kept in her back pocket before closing the hood. She didn't want to get grease on the paint job apparently.

She smiled over at Crystal with that sickeningly cute look I've come to realize is never going away, and really, I don't think I want it to. It seemed to make Charlie who she is. "Well Crystal, she said, It's not MY standards! And until it's up to MY standards, it's not good enough!" I laughed and looked over at Crystal. "I think I like this girl." I said with a smug little grin on my face. I wasn't't' sure if it was the fact that she used almost the exact same line I would have used, or, if it was the fact that she made Crystal shut up. Which was an extremely hard task to accomplish.

"Yeah cause you two are exactly alike!" Crystal stated, rolling her eyes as she turned and walk away in a huff.

"What are you talking about?" I said, turning sharply to face her.

"HEY!" I called after her as I turned and chased her back into the house.

"What do you mean, we're exactly alike? We're nothing alike! HEY! Are you even listening to me!?" I chased her all the way back into our living room. At that point, I thought it was all just fun and games. So, I snatched a hold of her arm by the shoulder and spun her around, giving her a playful shove.

"So what's this ~~shit~~ about me being just like that lil sissy bitch out there huh!? HUH!?" I shoved her playfully once more. I never saw it coming. What happened next that is. Crystal lunged forward with all the speed I seen her use during the corp run and grabbed me by my throat. She picked my body up off the floor and slammed my back up against the wall. The force of my body hitting the wall nearly knocked the breath right out of me. It caused the few pictures we had on the wall to come crashing to the floor shattering under the force. I didn't' understand what I did. I was just playing with her.

"The hell is yer ~~fucking~~ problem you ~~crazy~~ ~~fucking bitch~~!? Let me go!" I gagged as I tried to pry her hand away from my neck. I couldn't even break her grip with my cyber arm. She had me at her mercy right now. She just glared at me. It was as if she wanted to beat the shit out of me right there and then. She didn't' say anything and just let me down. She turned sharply and stomped away.

"Pop a fucking Midol ya frigg'n Pre-Menstrual syndrome bitch! I was only frag'n play'n ya uppity bitch! Damnit! GET BACK HERE!" I screamed after her. I could only imagine what Charlie thought outside. The truth was, I really didn't want her to come back. For the first time. I was afraid of someone. And of all people, I was afraid of Crystal. I kept asking myself. "Why did she lash out at me like that?" "Did I really piss her off that bad?" I was only kidding! I didn't see her for the rest of the night. I fell asleep on the couch for the first time since I could remember.

Chapter 5
Innocence Lost

August 28th
2060 New Seattle

Redmond Barrens District, Raven's Apartment
15:03:12pm

It was a slow day. I had little to do other than tinker with my ammo and weapons a bit while Crystal was away. I remember hearing Charlie rouse herself outside and start to work on my car again. I couldn't help but continue to be troubled about what Crystal had said the night before. It wasn't' even so much what she said, but how angry she became when I confronted her about it. I was only joking with her, but she seemed so very adamant about me and Charlie being so much alike. I wasn't anything like Charlie...was I? Did she mean by how green we were? How both of us were still new to this running stuff? By how precise we were in our trade? Like I am with my guns and Charlie is with her cars? Or was it how innocent and wimpy Charlie seemed to be? "I'm not weak! "....am I?" I found myself questioning my own existence at this point. Questioning the very meaning behind everything Crystal had said and done to me so far.

Like, when she held me...did she...I mean was she into me? Or did she just consider me like..."a kid sister"? I didn't' understand. I remember Charlie walking into the house to get something to eat and drink. She was talking to me about my car. I didn't even hear her. It wasn't' that I was trying to be rude or trying to ignore her. Nor was it that I wasn't interested in what she had to say about my car. I couldn't shake this feeling that something was wrong with Crystal. Ever since she jacked out of that terminal outside Brackhaven, something was weird about her and she hadn't stopped acting odd ever since. Why was it so upsetting that I DIDN'T want to be like Charlie!?

Finally Charlie went back outside. I sort of felt bad that I had pretty much ignored her the whole time she was inside eating and trying to tell me about my car. I continued to drink and smoke myself into a coma. I eventually fell asleep on the couch, again, out of boredom. Yeah, not so great for my sore neck. I remember my dream. It was strange, maybe the 12 pack I just drank was doing it to me but it was so graphic. Almost as if I was actually experiencing the dream. I remember, it was dark at first then there was a bright flash and I was looking up at a tile ceiling. I couldn't move my arms and legs. It wasn't like they were strapped down, it was almost as if they were not even there! I tried to sit up but my head was strapped down. My eyes moved frantically, back and forth, from one side of the room to the other. I was alone, strapped to a table in some room. The bright white light above my head was blinding, I could barely see anything for its blazing radiance. As my eyes grew more focused

I could tell it was a hospital room of sort. There were machines, not just typical hospital equipment, but drones and robots, moving about the room, cleaning, and doing maintenance in the room around me. I remember voices, distant at first but drawing nearer and nearer! I did not recognize these voices but I felt I had heard them before...at one time in my life. I struggled again against what I thought were restraints, but there were none..."Why can't I move!?" I said to myself. My heart began to race. I could hear it, beating, in my ears. Lub dub, lub dub, lub dub. Its pace, quickening as my senses slowly returned to me. Then, I heard the voices again. This time, more clearly someone...some..THING was talking to me!

"Ah...I see our "guest" is awake!" The voice was dark and cold. As if all sense of compassion and sincerity for my disposition was lacking in him. But something else had replaced this human emotion. Something..fake. Something...synthetic. His voice was almost mechanical. I tried to see who it was that was talking to me.
"Who are you!? Why am I here!? What is this about!" What the hell is going on!?" I spoke to the machine voice. There was no answer. No condolence for my fear which began to grow. And I was left with the sound of my heart beat again, beating...faster and faster. Lub dub, lub dub, lub dub, lub dub.
"Hello!? Who's there!? ANSWER ME

DAMNIT! What is going on!" Again I shouted into the sterile room, my body still not responding, I couldn't even wiggle my toes. "Why can't I move my body!?" I shouted again, above the pounding of my own heart. Lub dub, lub dub lub dub lub dub lub dub.

"I think our "guest" wants to know what we have done to her? Should we show her?" A robotic voice answered my cries from the darkness of the room. Then another, even colder, more distant voice answered that one. It sent chills up my spine.

"Hmmm...Show her! Show her what she has become!"

"What I have become...?!" I asked then felt what at first I thought was the room shifting. I soon realized, as my eyes darted around, that the table I was on was shifting, slowly, moving up. As if I was going to be dropped onto my feet which I still could not feel. My heart raced, lubdublubdublubdublubdublubdublubdub, faster and faster as the blinding light left my eyes and they began to focus before me was what appeared to be a mirror but it was a one way window. My side was the reflective side. Slowly my eyes came back into focus. At first I could not see myself then, slowly I beheld a site which made my heart beat stop. In the mirror I faced a reflection of myself I could not bare. I could not move my arms and legs because they weren't connected to my body anymore! I was strapped to a table by my neck, my upper body was no longer clothed nor did it possess any skin at all! My torso had been completely replaced with a cyber-body. My arms were gone as were my legs! Even my lower torso had been hacked off leaving only a lower portion of my spine. My eyes grew wide and I began to breath heavily, did I even have any lungs!? I could no longer hear my heart beat. I no longer had a heart beat! My heart was gone!

"Wh...what have you done to me!?" I gasped out in horror. I couldn't breath! Oh god! Did they take my lungs too! I thought to myself. "Oh but you haven't even seen the best part!" The mechanical voice came again. As I looked around to try and find the owner of this voice I saw another site which made me sick. Near the mirror in tubes, preserved, was my body! It was...me! I was actually staring at myself in a pickle jar! My body had been stripped of its clothing and cut apart piece by piece! My skull had been shaved and the top part removed.
"My brain!? The hell did you sickos due with my brain!?" I screamed. I wanted to vomit. I couldn't vomit! Oh god they took my stomach too!? Then I heard the colder voice again. "Look more closely Raven." It said with a hiss. I was afraid to but out of some strange sick curiosity I moved my eyes back to the mirror. My skull had been cut open and wires had been placed into my brain!? No, they had completely replaced my

skull! They were wiring my brain into this new body!

"No...I shook my head, as best I could, bolted to a cold operating table, my soul completely at the mercy of some mad man. NOOOOOO!!!!!" I screamed, the only thing left of me was my eyes. The voice came again from the darkness, then, then I knew where I had heard this voice before. It was the voice in the back of my mind! The same voice the night of my corp run. It spoke in another hiss, with no emotion, no care, no remorse at what they were doing to me.
"Now, it's time for the finishing touches! Once we finish putting you together and reprogramming your brain, you will be our puppet. Our own personal doll! You will do whatever we say!" Just then the machines in the room began to move. Making their way toward me, I squirmed against restraints I could do nothing to break! The machines converged on me as I screamed in terror. I shouted;
"I don't want to be a machine! NO! PLEASE NO! I don't want to be a machine!!!!!!"

But no one helped me, it was so real. I could swear I felt them connecting the cyber arms to me. Maybe it was still my new nervous system acting up, or just phantom pains from my old arm. but I could even swear I felt my lower body being connected. Slowly the machines moved away from me and the clamps and wires released from

my body. The heavy metal crashed to the floor
like a pile of scrap metal. I slowly began to pull
my new form up onto its new mechanical limbs. I
could not feel....anything! My feet no longer
could feel the cold marble floor. My neck and
back no longer felt the soft texture of my hair, I
was crying, but my cheeks could not feel the heat
of the tears, nor my heart the pain of losing my
body. I stood and looked at my hands, they were
all metal! Skeletal remains of what I used to be!
My beautiful hands and skin now hard wire and
circuitry. I tried to touch my face and my body
but I could feel nothing! Tears poured from my
eyes, hatred filled my soul, anger, rage, pain, not
just from my new body, but the loss of everything
that I felt made me whole.

I slowly raised my head, my elfish eyes fixing
on the mirror. I swear, I could see two figures,
both, with glowing green cyber eyes beyond the
other side one male one female. "...how...could
you....?" I said, my new body finding its new
strength, shaking from the rage and self-disgust I
felt welling up inside my empty hollow chest. I
stood there a long moment. There was no answer,
no redemption for the pain I now felt that I could
not explain.
"HOW COULD YOU!!!!!???" I screamed to the
dark silhouettes beyond that mirror. Demanding
closure, demanding something for my pain. Still
nothing, they stood there in defiance to my anger,
to my pain and rage. I screamed flexing my metal

shell, horrific blades extending from the upper hand of each arm, as I was crying out for reconciliation.

"HOW COULD YOU DO THIS TO ME!!!!???" Still nothing the darkness inside me grew as I felt my soul itself grow empty and dark until even it could feel no longer. But still the tears came still the rage filled me, till that is all there was. Then once more I heard the dark hiss. This time, as if from all around me, as if all the machines were speaking to me in unison.

"But Raven, do you not feel stronger now? Faster? More powerful? You will never age now, you will never have to eat, never have to sleep, you will never feel pain, or sorrow, or suffering ever again. You are immortal now. Do you not feel it?" The voice sent a chill of cold up my now cybernetic spine. Like poison creeping into my veins or an icy wind brushing your skin. Still, all that I could feel inside was hatred, rage, and sorrow. I just wanted to break and burn down everything...EVERYTHING in my path. I had never felt so dark in my life. I screamed toward the figure which was now all I could see other than the red forming over my eyes.

"FEEL!!?? I can't FEEL ANYTHING anymore!" I leapt forward with an animalistic rage that I had never knew I could muster. The metal body was heavy but it was much stronger and faster than my elfish one. I was as fast as Crystal now, if not faster. I tore through the machines in front of me like a wild beast and shattered through the glass mirror before me. I sank the cyber blades of my metal hands into the dark figure before me till I felt them bite into flesh, ripping, tearing, rending dismembering the flesh before me. I was no longer human...I was a beast...a beast made of metal parts and wires. As I tore into the humanoid figure before me, I heard the other's voice. Still dark, and empty but now..more human than before. I slowly stood up from my prey as she began to laugh. It was Crystal's voice!

I lifted my new burdenous weight from her body and she rose in almost a super natural fashion, like a black shadow looming out of the ground. The room I had entered was darker than the clinic and the mirror I crashed through seemed so distant now. As if I was no longer in the mortal realm. As she rose she laughed so darkly it caused me to slowly back away. Suddenly, fear now filled my empty shell. She cackled evilly, her green cyber eyes growing wider. Soon, I could see her she...she was me!?
"Wh...what the hell are you!?" I stuttered as suddenly my cyber body no longer functioned and I fell to the floor immobile unable to move, my rage now leaving me, leaving me empty! Empty and filled with fear.
"What am I you ask Raven?" The figure spoke as it moved toward me. Its body was filled with holes from where I had attacked it, its skin mauled almost completely off its body. Underneath was

metal! Just like me!

"I am you!" She said as she moved like a blur a black shadow following behind her. Her cold metal hand grabbing my neck and lifting me off the ground. She picked my heavy cyber body up with one hand holding me there staring into my eyes with those dark green cyber eyes.

"I am everything you want! I am everything you desire, I am your pain, I am your rage, I am your sorrow, I am your shadow, the dark voice that still lingers from your past in the back of your mind. I am the thing you call upon for strength when you have none! I am you, just as much as you are me. And I am everything you are about to become! Just as you are the mirror image of EVERYTHING you are about to leave behind!"

She laughed darkly as she reached her other hand up, its metal bones morphing into a talon-like claw which began to slowly rotate like a saw coming toward my eyes.

"There's only one thing left for you to lose! Those innocent little eyes of yours!" The whirling blade grew closer and closer to my eyes I tried to fight her grip loose of my throat but I couldn't fight her, she was stronger than me, faster than me...better than me.

"No! No please no not that! ANYTHING BUT THAT!!" I pleaded sorrowfully, my pathetic pleases only bringing the sadistic doppelganger more joy.

"Oh ho? What happened to that confidence I saw but a moment ago? All that anger, all that rage, all the hatred! IS THAT THE EXTENT OF

YOUR STRENGTH? My copy laughed in sadistic glee as I screamed in agony. The blades cutting into my face removing from me my last bit of humanity. There was no heart beat anymore, no breath, no tears just blood and pain! I screamed and clawed at her metal arm until I awoke screaming in pain. Apparently my cigarette had fallen from my mouth and burnt a hole through my jeans leaving a blister on my leg. "It was...just a dream...?" I said to myself, my heart racing in my chest my body shaking as sweat poured from my body. "Or...was it?" I looked over myself. And very closely at the cyber arm on right side of my body. I had heard of premonitions before. But I always chalked it up to superstitious mumbo jumbo and coincidences and other crap like that. One thing was certain though. It left me feeling very disturbed. No sooner did I awake with a fright from my nightmarish vision than did the front door of the apartment slam open. It scared the living be Jesus out of me! I fell off the couch and into a pile of old beer cans with a crash. It was Crystal coming in from wherever she had gone. She looked over at me and blinked as if surprised she caught me off guard.

"What the heck are you doing lying around Raven? Shouldn't you be getting ready for Charlie's job tonight?" She said to me in a very calm tone. It was very strange, considering the night before she was fuming mad it seemed. "I already did everything I could do for tonight! I gruffed at her as I sat up rubbing my head after crashing into the pile aluminum cans. I mean you've been gone all day! The hell have you been?"

Crystal simply chuckled as a few beer cans tumbled down around me. She didn't seem at all upset anymore. Almost as if, she was a different person. She walked in and set a bag on our living room table which was littered with random newspapers, mostly the local crime reports and information on the corps and local STAR activity. Some old empty Chinese containers, empty clips, and a survival knife. The bag spilled over and a few boxes of shells fell out along with a piece of equipment I had never seen before. Crystal turned to face me with a smile and replied, "I was out getting a few supplies for our mission. It's not much, but it should help us out. I stood up, brushing cans off my lap and walked over to the table, examining the items she had purchased. There were several boxes of ammunition of different gauges for our weapons, stim patches, and some first aid supplies. The object I didn't' recognize, was a small black box that almost looked like an old world AC adapter. It didn't have two prongs though, only one. The other end had a wire that came out of it, similar to the metal end of an old fashioned cell phone charger.

"What's this?" I asked Crystal, holding the object up as I inspected it. Crystal moved over and took the cubic object from my hand and slowly, slide her cool pale hand up the length of my left cyber arm, pushing the main length of my sleeve up. I shivered, not just cause her hand was cold, but I was still a little scared from my nightmare and it felt nice to have a soft hand on my cold carbon steel alloy arm. It seemed to make the knot that was making my stomach so sick go away. Even if only for a little bit.

"It's an Instinct Link, she replied to me. It connects your brain directly to an instinct link compatible weapon, like your 9mm. It attaches to a cyber-arm or cyber brain. I figured since you're stuck with that arm, it might as well be useful right?" She spoke softly to me as she connected the Instinct Link to my arm. It fit snuggly into the back of the arm and the cord laced down into the palm of my hand. It pinched a little when she first snapped it in place but after it was securely installed in my cyber arm, I didn't' even notice it.

"Wow, I said, slightly impressed at the fact that this cyber implant was very light and actually useful. How does it work?" I asked as I looked up at her eyes which were almost shimmering as they gazed back into my own. I felt my cheeks flush slightly.

"It's actually quite simple really." She replied as softly as before. I couldn't help but notice her pale red lips as she spoke. They looked so soft and her face was so close to my own. I remember biting my own lip trying to stay focused on what she was saying. Her hand slid down my arm again to the palm of my cyber hand. "This end is placed in the Instinct Link connection on any Instinct Link compatible gun. Once attached, the gun will fire quicker, aim easier, switch firing modes faster, as well as become easier to reload. The Instinct Link connects either directly to the brain, or, directly to the neural interface of your cyber limb which is connected directly to your nervous system. Increasing your proficiency with an Instinct Gun greatly." It was indeed a very handy device to have around. And as Crystal had said, since I was stuck with this cyber limb, I might as well make full use of it. I knew Crystal had some cyber ware installed, but for the most part, I couldn't really see any of it other than her data jack.

"How do you know so much about cyber ware Crystal?" I asked, feeling her soft icy fingers in the palm of my cyber hand. I felt my head moving closer to hers. At first I tried to hold it back then I noticed for each bit that my own lips moved towards hers, hers moved equally toward mine. I felt my heart beating faster again, a relief to hear after such a horrid dream. And, a feeling of warmth enter my body that had been long missed for some time now. I felt my thighs quiver slightly as I slowly, almost involuntarily moved toward her. Our eyes were stuck on each other and neither of us could pull away from the other. I remember my cyber hand suddenly grasped her hand as if by a will all its own. We both gasped.

"I...I'm sorry! I still haven't quite got used to this new nervous system!" I stuttered to try to come up with an explanation for my actions that even I myself could not understand. Crystal merely smiled, and slowly laced her fingers through mine and clasped her hand around my own. I looked down then back up into her icy blue eyes which still had me so mesmerized. Crystal's head tilted slightly and she spoke softly to me again,
"It's alright. I don't mind."

Our lips moved closer to one another, I felt my eyes beginning to close and my pulse quicken. The knot in my stomach loosened more but was replaced with butterflies. I held my breath awaiting the moment that our lips would touch. Then, as if being awoken from another dream, the door flung open, yet again, and Charlie burst in yelling
"I'M ALL FINISHED!" I jumped almost straight out of my seat and fell over backwards out of my chair. I couldn't see Crystal's face so I have no idea how she reacted to Charlie's typically sudden and impeccable timing. Charlie looked down at me, apparently, she either didn't' notice what Crystal and I were up to, or she was just oblivious to it as usual. "Oh, Raven, are you alright?" Charlie asked in her typical innocent way. I grumbled under my breath at her as I stood back up, lifting my chair up off the floor.
"Yes Charlie, I'm perfectly fine. Thank you for the wonderful news and also the incredibly wonderful mood kill!" I set the chair back down and sat, informally, with the back of the chair against my chest and looked over at her. Crystal

had no real expression on her face as if nothing ever happened.

"So, Charlie, I said, getting my mind back onto the subject at hand, what's the sitch with this run?"

Chapter 6
Innocence Lost pt 2

August 29th 2060
New-Seattle

Neo-Everett District, 21:04:00pm

Our car pulled up to the upscale vehicle repair shop outside their dump site where they kept all the scrap metal and vehicle parts. We cut the lights there and got out of the car.
"Everybody remember what they're supposed to do?" I asked in a low voice as we loaded our weapons. I took my Berretta this time. I wanted to see just what this Instinct Link could do. I was carrying my Desert Eagle in my right hand. I really couldn't fire it one handed, but I only had one Instinct Link and my Desert Eagle wasn't designed to be used with Instinct Links.
"I'm all set!" Crystal replied as she checked the strap that held her katana to her back. She was armed with her usual mini AK's and her trusty katana on her back. She chose darker clothes for this run. Her pants were black denim and her top was a black leather ballistics vest with no sleeves cut strategically in the front. She had her hair tied up in a bun. "As ready as I'll ever be." Charlie replied. She wore just her over alls and that old beat up tee she always wore.
"Alright, let's do this then! I was wearing my usual. Faded red denim pants, and my plated

leather jacket. We split up into groups. Crystal and I moved through the junk yard toward the rear of the garage. Charlie made her way toward the main entrance. I was trying to keep my head clear. Only my second run and it was another big one. I was trying to recall all of Charlie's story so I'd have some idea of what to expect.

"The place we're hitting is now an affiliate of Federated-Boeing in the Everett area. They produce some of the smaller armored vehicles that the bigger Federated-Boeing industries contract out to smaller companies. They may not be very big, but they make a pretty decent sized pay check. However, back in its younger years, that garage belonged to my father. But back then, it was much smaller and a lot more friendly to those that were less fortunate. At the time, we fixed cars, trucks, jeeps, and some small hover vehicles. According to the news feeds, Federated-Boeing bought our garage after making us a very "generous" offer. That was for the faint of heart. Actually what really happened was a negotiator from their company kept paying us a visit. At first, it was once a month, asking my father if he wanted to sell. My father never wanted to sell." Charlie paused a moment to take a drink of her soy-caf in front of her then continued with her story.

"My mother, on the other hand, preferred that my father go work for Boeing instead of wasting his time with his own business. I suppose her intentions were good, but she just didn't have the same ideals as my father. Ever since I was able to hold a wrench I would help my father in the garage. That's where I spent most of my time. My mother hated the idea that her little girl was spending all her time in a musty dirty old garage. She wanted me to go to school and make something of myself. I guess I maybe should have taken up something to do in my off time. But no sense worrying about the past now. At first, I think Federated-Boeing didn't think much of us. And that's what my father chose to believe. "What concern would a multibillion Credit company like Federated-Boeing have with a couple thousand cred business like our own? He used to say." I listened diligently to Charlie's story. I may not have really liked her, but every runner has a story to tell. The least any of us can do is listen. I looked around a pile of scrap at Crystal and nodded. She nodded as well, in reply to my nod. I motioned with my hand to move forward and we both moved at the same time, moving between piles of rubble and scrap toward the building. I continued to recall Charlie's tale as I worked my way through the maze of broken down cars and miniature hover crafts.

"That's what my father chose to believe. And for a while, he was right. Our Boeing visitor came month after month and each month, he was sent away empty handed. I didn't think much of him and neither did my father. And each time my mother begged and pleaded with my father to sell and each time he refused. And so it went for many years. We grew as a family and our little garage grew too. Nothing much changed until one fateful day my father discovered a way to create better more efficient fuel for ground vehicles. What did you expect? I mean, we played with vehicles every day. It was merely a matter of time before we figured it out. Suddenly, our small garage started to become very, VERY popular very fast! We got our own set of gas pumps and people from all around Seattle and from other parts of the UCAS began to show up at our little garage. My mother finally decided that maybe she had been a little too quick to judge. But of course, our discovery didn't' escape the eyes of Federated-Boeing either. This could very well be their ticket to the Lime Light if they could get their grubby little hands on it. So, once again we were visited by our friendly Federated-Boeing negotiator who kept trying to get my father to sell before. But now, now they were a little bit more persistent. The visits became more frequent. From once a month to ever 3 weeks then every other week then once a week, soon, my father was seeing Boeing lawyers every day. They were like regular customers. Only the kind that you wish would never come back again."

Charlie's story was like many others you'd hear from a typical runner. I thought to myself, as I rounded a corner in time to hear two dogs growling in the distance. I stopped and leaned down behind an old rusted car frame, looking out over the distance. A normal human wouldn't' have been able to see jack in the darkness of the scrap heap. But elves have low light vision. And I was no different than any other elf. I saw them in the distance. Two Dobermans prancing back and forth near a pile of old motors. They were junk yard dogs. Put there to keep kids out of the junk yard and thieves from stealing the useful parts that were still in the junk yard. I figured I had to be close to the main garage. I looked around but I couldn't see Crystal anywhere. I figured she had moved on.

"Shit!" I cussed under my breath. I remember thinking that a good ear bud radio would be an excellent investment for future runs. We had to sell the ones we had from the first run to make ends meet. Even if we still had them, we only had the two at the time.

"C'mon think Raven think!" I muttered to myself as I watched the two dogs stalk back and forth and back and forth. I knew they were just waiting for me to step out from behind my hiding place so they could turn me into an elfy chew toy. It was too risky to try and sneak around them. Then I remembered the Instinct Link that Crystal had installed in my arm earlier. I reached into my inside pocket of my leather and pulled out a small black case. I opened it and pulled out a long metallic tube. It was the silencer for my Berretta. I knew very well I couldn't just start firing at these two dogs without silencing my weapon or I was going to give us away. And each shot was going to have to count! Besides, the longer I crouched here waiting, the further ahead of me Crystal was getting.

I slid my left hand into my back pocket and pulled out my partially crumpled pack of Turkish Wides. I shook one smoke slowly up and pulled it free with my lips. I slid the pack slowly back into the rear pocket of my old red denim jeans and slowly reached into the top pocket of my leather. I produced my favorite Zippo lighter, which I flicked open and lit my cigarette. I took a long slow drag then slowly exhaled as I turned my focus back on the dogs which were now stationary. They had stopped when they saw the glint from my Zippo's flint. "Well, at least they're not pacing back and forth anymore." I whispered with a grin to myself.
"Let's just see how useful this new Instinct Link really is." I said as I slowly roll my Turkish wide along my pink lips with my tongue to the side of my mouth. I tilted my head slightly to the side, leaving both eyes open and slowly moved to a kneeling position as I carefully raised my berretta to eye level, leaving my Desert Eagle securely hidden in my shoulder holster under my jacket. I watched the dogs as they watched me. Slowly

puffing on my cigarette, smoke curling off the lit end. The two Dobermans slowly began to move toward me. I watched them as they drew nearer and nearer to my position. I knew they could smell me now. They were just waiting for the right moment to strike. But I showed no fear as I slowly took a firm two handed grip on my Berretta, feeling my heart slow a little.

"Well, here goes nothing!" I said to myself as I squeezed off the first two shots. Any other time, trying to shoot two dogs in the dead of night with a small hand gun with all that junk around me would have been a pretty difficult shot. But, with the Instinct Link Crystal gave me, it made the job so much easier. The first Doberman went down like a ton of bricks. Both shots piercing the big dog's thick skull. The other dog started to charge me. Every rational fiber of my being was screaming run! But there was that voice again in the back of my mind. As if something was telling me to stay put. Saying,
"Wait for it....wait for it..." The voice kept repeating as the dog charged closer and closer. Its beady eyes glinting in the star light, its jowls dripping with saliva. Its fangs were barred and its growls of anger grew louder and louder as the big dog drew closer to me. But still I waited by some will not my own. Puffing nervously on my cigarette. Then, out of no-where, just as I thought I was goner, the huge beast leapt at me its fangs dripping snarling with primal fury. Its jaws

poised for my neck. I lifted the gun and fired three more shots and, with a yipe of pain, the dog crashed head first onto the frame of the car and tumbled over dead at my feet. I could hear my heart beating again. Lub dub lub dub lub dub. I took a big drag from my smoke and stood up flicking the cigarette away. I looked down at the two dead Dobermans at my feet and breathed a sigh of relief.

"That worked better than I had hoped!" I said with a great feeling of accomplishment and started through the junk heaps again, trying to catch up with Crystal who was now a few legs ahead. My mind wandered back to Charlie's story once again.

"Yeah they made us a couple of "generous" offers. However no matter what they offered, my father refused to sell. He told them he wanted something to give to his children one day. He told them that this business was part of his family. And like a family at first, he was scared, he didn't know what he was doing but he pretended he did. And then his family got bigger and he was faced with a difficult decision. Whether to merge his family with another one. It was a big decision. He wanted the best for it and he felt that merging it with Corporate Boeing would have been a huge mistake. Probably the biggest of his life. He was wrong. The biggest mistake of his life was refusing to sell." I remember being touched and moved by Charlie's words at that moment. I finally felt like maybe, we actually did have something in common. Even if that was all.

I rounded another heap of scrap. I saw Crystal lurking around the corner of the main garage. As I crept closer she turned toward me and waved me over. I moved quickly but quietly to her position. Staying low as I got up beside her.

"The hell took you so long Raven?!" She asked in a stern whisper. Turning her head back to survey the surrounding area.

"I got held up by a couple of junk yard dogs." I replied as I scanned the surrounding area as well checking the clip in my berretta.

"Don't worry, I added, I took care of them." Crystal looked down at me with a smirk.

"Take it that Instinct Link is working well for ya then?" I grinned back up at her, sliding the clip back into my nine. "Yeah, thanks a load! That could have turned out a lot worse without it."

Crystal looked around one last time then whispered down to me, keeping her eyes on the door.

"Alright, Charlie should already be inside. Let's move!"

"Kay!" I replied quick and simple then followed her lead to the door. My back against the wall opposite to her on the other side of the door. I recalled more of what Charlie had told us.

"His biggest mistake ever! One night, when we had closed up shop for the evening, we were all sitting around the TV watching a movie when, suddenly, we heard a huge explosion outside. My father rushed outside. I wanted to follow him but he made me stay inside with my mother. I remember watching helplessly from the screen door. Apparently a group of runners that Boeing hired had got into our Garage. I guess they were just supposed to smash up the joint. But one of them must of accidentally ruptured one of the gas pumps and a single spark set them a-blaze."

"By the time my father got outside, the fire had already spread to the majority of the garage, he was trying to save what little he could and the runners saw him. Panicked by the fact that they pretty much already hosed this run, they shot him. My father died almost instantly. To make matters worse the fire had begun to spread to our house." So many runners' stories sound the same, I recalled in my mind. Most of us were all just average every-day Joes just trying to get by. When the corps step in and completely turn our lives upside down. No wonder runners detest them with every fiber of their being. Crystal and I made eye contact again. Mentally, I suppose, we were making sure we were both ready. I nodded to her and she nodded to me. Slowly she turned the knob, it was unlocked.

"Charlie must of got the doors open." Crystal whispered lightly as she slowly pushed the door open.

"Good." I replied. "Then so far, everything is going according to plan."

Once inside we assessed our surroundings. This place was frag'n huge! However this wasn't necessarily a bad thing. If you've ever been in a large garage, you know that there are tons of metal wracks around. Usually spaced just far enough apart for a person to fit through. But close enough that light gun fire would be blocked. Crystal and I tried to keep a rack of car parts in between the two of us. Giving us both ample cover. As we crept forward we noticed there were still a few goons lurking about. We did our best to subdue the ones we saw. Using stealth and guile, we put them down with ease. We didn't really want to kill them. We just gave them all mild concussions! Once we got toward the back end of the garage, near the offices, I tried to remember the reason we were here.

"Though we don't own that garage anymore, I remember them keeping the layout of it pretty much the same." Charlie laid out a blue print of the original garage in front of us on our rickety old kitchen table. It was scattered with bullets gun parts, and now tools. All of which she used to help hold down the edges of the blue print. It looked old as shit! Like she'd had it for years. The paper it was drawn on was so worn from being folded, rolled, crumpled, and all around carried around on every part of her body imaginable that it more closely resembled something you'd wipe your ass on.
"There's a safe in the far back of the garage, she pointed out the location on the blue print, inside is where we used to keep the week's take. We

usually kept five days-worth of earnings in it then, on Friday, we'd take a money bag to the bank and deposit it. However, we also always tried to keep aprox 1500 creds in there for change and anything else we may need it for."

I raised my eyebrow giving the small girl a doubtful look.
"I dun mean to sound ungrateful or anything Charlie but, 1500 creds aint even gonna cover HALF our rent." The small grimy girl looked up at me with a slightly puzzled look. As if she didn't understand a word I just said.
"Umm..ok?" She stared at me with those big eyes from behind those nerdy glasses. I felt the vein in my forehead beginning to throb and the peaceful look on my face begin to turn to irritancy. Her eyes suddenly got really big. The way they usually do when she knows I'm about to yell at her and she squeaked lightly at me.
"Err...they probably have about 10,000 creds on hand in their vault now!" She shrank back away from me for bit till she seen my annoyance give way to, well, greed.

"TEN THOUSAND CREDITS!?" I exclaimed, causing the already nervous Charlie to topple out of her chair.
"Now your frag'n talk'n!!" Aside from Charlie and my own comical love/hate relationship, she was on to something. We were already headed toward the back office when we were greeted by a not so promising sight. We saw Charlie being detained from behind by a big, heavily cybered, mechanic. She was surrounded by four other

mechanics all partially cybered holding an assortment of weapons from wrenches, to pipes, to even hunting knives. Apparently they had caught her snooping around and were about to let her know just how they felt about it.

"SHIT!" I cussed under my breath again, looking toward Crystal who was as well cussing at the situation.

Granted yeah, we have guns they don't, at least none that we can see. But starting a fire fight in this garage would draw too much attention as well as could explode some caustic chemicals.

Thinking fast, Crystal reached up onto one of the metal wracks, pulling down a large part of what looked like a transmission, she whipped it at the back of the one goon's head. She clocked him good as he went down hard, a growing pool of crimson blood forming underneath him.

"Who threw Dat!?" The heavily cybered mechanic, holding Charlie at knife point, belted out in fractured English. We didn't move.

"C'mon outta dere who eva you ere!" We still didn't budge.

"C'mon out ya chicken shit! I wanna see y'ere face!"

Slowly Crystal stood up I looked up at her like she was crazy! Shaking my head swiftly and mouthing "The hell are you doing?! Are ya trying to get yourself killed!?" She shook her head at me mouthing in response,

"Don't worry I got this. I'll be fine!" I gave her a stern, irritated look, mouthing back.

"Don't give me that! This is no time to..." But before I could finish my silent objection, the mechanic shouted crudely back in his butchered grammar. He had apparently seen Crystal's silhouette.

"Ya, I see yas over there ya goofy bas'tard! Git ye'r ass out he're! I wanna see who tinks he's got some big ballz!" Slowly, her heels clicking on the cold plascrete floor, every step of the way, Crystal glided out into the dim light. Her sleek figure moving smoothly through the shadows till she was in the light. Her clothes clung to her form. I could only imagine what these pigs were thinking.

All of them were staring at her like wolves who just watched a stray fawn stumble upon their pack. They were chuckling and grinning darkly at her. I remember I had to swallow hard not to yell at her. And that only made the knot in my stomach tighten. The cybered mechanic was the first to speak of the 3 remaining.

"Ey ey! What's this!? A dame!? Ey bois, you see dis ere? Ol Frank dere was knocked out a by a broad!?" His references to women were vulgar and excruciatingly ill mannered. He obviously didn't think much of Crystal. He taunted her as if she could never be his equal as he continued to badger her mercilessly.

"Ey, ey, doll face, dis broad ere a friend o' yours?" He pointed the tip of the blade toward Charlie's neck and I gripped the handle of my Desert Eagle tighter, gritting my teeth.

I could feel beads of sweat rolling down my cheek and neck. It took all my concentration not to kill this disgusting pig as he continued his demeaning rant!

"...Cause ya know, if she is, I might be persuaded to spare her ass. If yer willing to give me a lil sumthin in return. If ya know what I mean sweet cheeks?" Crystal remained silent, scanning the group of men. Watching them as they tapped their make-shift weapons in the palms of their grimy, grease and soot covered hands.

"Eh? Whatsa matta? Dontcha know how to talk?! Ah that's jus too bad. I guess I'll have to kill this lil bitch here den!" He began to press the tip of the blade into Charlie's throat and I began to pull my Desert Eagle from my leather. I was just about to stand up when I heard Crystal finally speak.

"Oh I know quite well how to speak, thank you very much." Crystal began, her words cutting into the pig like a freshly sharpened axe.

"I was simply taken a-back by the fact that you could even pronounce the word "persuaded" without horridly butchering it like you've done with every other word you're small brain has attempted to pronounce!" I had to stifle a snicker. I was thinking just the same thing. However, Crystal wasn't laughing. Her eyes were cold and dark and her face was stern. Her posture had grown very straight and poised. Her arms were crossed over her bust as she glared down the four men with great disdain. The three men looked to one another then toward the cyber mechanic, who was apparently their boss. He looked from one to the

other of them then back to Crystal. Apparently
not accustomed to a battle of wits.

"Oh what?! Ya makin fun'eh the way I talk
now?! Well...well what the frag do you know ya
dumb bimbo broad?!" Once again the pig
resorted to trying to down play Crystal's obvious
feminine superiority. It didn't even phase her.
"Oh?" Crystal began, showing greater malice in
her words. Each one dripping with venom like a
poisonous cobra just waiting to strike.
"That's your come back? Demeaning comments
based upon my appropriate gender? Oh please!
You are pathetic! Okay I'll tell you what? How
about I make YOU a deal! You let the girl go,
apologize to her and myself, and I promise I
won't rip your balls off through your ass!" I
could feel the cold off of that comment! With that
last comment she had successfully de-
masculinized this pig. Did she really think that he
would let Charlie go? I honestly doubted it but
you never know about Crystal.

"What the hell-ere you guys doin? Stand'n
around ere tak'n that shit from some dumb broad!?
KILL ER! Beat da bitch right outta er!" He
waved the knife around carelessly at his fellow
workers. Ordering them to do his bidding. And
they fell in line intently like little soldiers do. At
first, the one with the wrench and the cyber arm
came after Crystal. He left himself wide open too.
Hitting the wrench off the palm of his flesh hand.
"Yer mine ya lil bitch!" He said, his grammar
almost as bad as his boss'. Slowly I watched
Crystal. She didn't move, only watched him

approach. Then he swung the wrench in a strong, fast, downward motion toward her. She quickly moved her head to the side while reaching out to grab his wrist and with a swift twist and quick upward thrust she snapped both the cyber wrist and elbow of his arm! I watched him drop the wrench and before the heavy metal tool could even hit the floor, she rotated her body, using her back and hips, with the torque on his already damaged limb, to lift him up and toss him into the trunk of a nearby car. It swiftly closed on top of him afterwards.

"What ya gonna let some bitch get da betta of ya!? Whats da matta witchu all!? She's just a broad! De're two of ya and y'er men! GET HER!!!" The two other men rushed Crystal from both sides. One with a lead pipe and the other an old tow chain. As I watched them converge on her, I began to remember the rest of Charlie's story she had told us.

"The fire had already spread to our house. My mother and I barely had time to get out before our home, the home I had grown up in, the home I had lived in all my life, our home, my home, was completely engulfed in flames! The next day, after the fire company had put out the flames which had completely destroyed everything...EVERYTHING! All our possessions, our life, everything we owned, even my father, had been engulfed by that fire. The Boeing lawyer came to us again. He expressed such heart-felt sympathy for our loss. I knew it was nothing more than an act, false sympathy for a fire their corrupt corporation had created to sweep away everything we loved. We had no choice. My mother sold all the assets of our company to Federated Boeing. They gave us 500,000 credits. Sure it was enough to get us back on our feet. But it could never replace what they had taken from us. From me."

The first strike came from the mechanic with the chain. He swung it out wide toward Crystal. She held up her arm and let the length of it wrap around her forearm. Using the chain, she pulled him toward her to block the strike from the lead pipe. It hit deep in the back of the guy's skull, knocking him unconscious almost instantly. She kicked him back off of her into a pile of scrap freeing the chain from his hand. The pipe came again. She flung the other end of the chain up into her hand and used it to catch and entangle the pipe. With a quick flick of her wrist and a twist, she disarmed the man and then flung the pipe up into his face, shattering the cyber eye he had. Partially blinded, he stumbled backward stunned. With the chain, Crystal wrapped up the man's arm and jerked him viciously toward her.

She turned her body again, causing his arm to be twisted and wrapped up in the chain. As he came forward, she continued into the turn, so his mid-section would strike her elbow. Having knocked the wind out of the man, she flung her head back into his nose, shattering the brittle cartilage inside. A fountain of dark red blood spewed from his nose. With another flip of her wrist, she wrapped the rest of the length of the chain up under his crotch and around his shoulder

Lilliana Annette Deeters

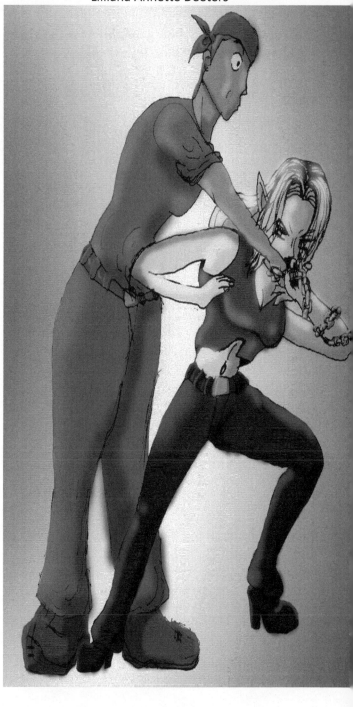

pinning his arm between his legs and causing him to be doubled over. And, with a swift pull, she flipped him three times in the air before he landed, face first, on the plascrete floor stone cold unconscious. She then turned her attention to their heavily cybered boss, who still had Charlie at knife point. She glared coldly at him, her stare so bitter, it could freeze the very soul.

"So, you gonna hide behind a defenseless girl all night? Or aren't you man enough to test your luck with "some dumb broad?" Her voice was icy cold and carried the sting of winter's frost on it.

The foul mouthed man began to look around frantically for an out. Not finding an easy way out, he held the blade of the knife flush against Charlie's neck and began to retreat back into the office. Taunting Crystal, feeling safe with his hostage and human shield.

"Oh I'd betchu'd like dat wouldn't ya bitch!? So ya's can bust me up like ya did my bois eh? Well FORGET IT! I aint dat stupid! I gots me a hostage! And I intend on use'n er to git outta-ere!"

"Damn you!" Crystal cursed at him, "LET HER GO YOU COWARDLY PIG!" The fat mechanic just laughed as he released one hand from Charlie to turn the door knob on the office door.

"Not dis time bitch!" He snorted back at her. Having had just about enough of being a human shield, Charlie took this opportunity to practice some of her own "Martial Arts".

Since the fat pig had released one arm from

around her, Charlie had just enough wiggle room to latch a hold of what little flesh and blood was left of his arm with her teeth. She bit down like a rabid fox escaping the jaws of a bear. She bit his arm so hard, she literally drew blood! The fat mechanic screamed, which gave her enough wiggle room to stamp down on his foot with the heel of her hard mechanic's boots. He let go of her like she was on fire, hopping up and down on one foot. Charlie fell on her ass, then scrambled on all fours toward Crystal like a child scurrying toward its mother. Once she got over to Crystal, Crystal put her arm around Charlie to shield her, taking her attention off the pig for just a second to make sure Charlie was safe.

"You okay Charlie girl?" Crystal asked. Charlie nodded with a reply,
"Yeah I'm fine." The mechanic, recovering from Charlie's child-like assault, brandished his knife and charged Crystal. She looked up just in time to dodge to the side, only to take a deep gash across her left upper arm which quickly began to bleed. She yelped in pain looking down at her arm then quickly returned her attention to the fat pig who was coming back with another slice. Crystal, some-how, managed to catch his arm, but he was obviously much stronger than the others. She was quickly losing the fight. By now, I was on my feet with my Desert Eagle pulled, cocked, and ready! The mechanic saw me come into light and responded with a dumb founded,
"Wha..??! Dere's another broad in ere!? The hell...?"

He didn't get to finish, because Charlie suddenly walloped him a good one in the back of the head with that lead pipe that had been still laying at her feet. The fat mechanic groaned in pain, giving Crystal enough time to get the knife out of his hand. She then gave him a swift kick in the old family jewels, which dropped him to his knees. I seized the moment, as soon as Crystal went down to one knee to doctor her arm, I leapt up and kicked the fat pig square in the jaw, sending him skidding across the floor and threw the office door. I instantly knelt down to make sure Crystal and Charlie were alright.

"You guys okay?" I asked, concerned at how deep Crystals cut was on her arm. I also questioned the cleanliness of that pig's hunting knife.

"Yeah... Crystal replied hoarsely, I'm alright. It's just a scratch. Charlie nodded, she herself only had a light cut on her neck from the edge of the knife being pressed so close to it.

"I'm okay too." Charlie replied weakly. I more closely inspected Crystal's arm, the cut was pretty deep. And the cut didn't look too godly if you know what I mean. "That looks pretty deep Crystal." I said with a grimace on my face.

"It's alright. I'll be fine." She tried to reassure me, but I wasn't buying it.

"Bull Shit! I responded, let me at least cover it till we can get you to a hospital." I took off my leather, dropping it to the floor behind me and tore a large portion of my top, leaving most of my stomach uncovered, and began to bandage Crystal's arm. She watched me quietly for a time

then said, flatly,
"You don't have to do this." I didn't look up at
her, I wanted to make sure her wound was
properly covered as I replied to her.
"Ah forget about it! We're partners. We gotta
look out for one another!" I looked up at her
softly. "Besides, it's the least I can do after what
you've done for me." I smiled at her.

She stared at me for a moment. And at first it
was kind of awkward. I thought maybe I
shouldn't have said anything. Then, suddenly,
she smiled back. She put her hand on my head
and rustled my hair a bit.
"Thanks Raven." She had a calm, gentle look in
her eyes. I blushed a little. Then just as the
moment began to get deeper, I heard a voice.
"...this aint ova! NOT BY A LONG SHOT!!" As
we looked up that fat pig was still standing! And
he had a sawed off in his hand! He was pretty
badly battered, but that shotgun was in rare form!
He had it pointed right at us. And at that distance,
he could have fragged the lot of us to kingdom
come! Charlie was not much of a shooter, and
Crystal's arm was in no shape to fire a gun! I
didn't think, hell I didn't even breath! All I did
was react! I shoved Crystal into Charlie with my
left arm, knocking them both out of the way, then
rolled toward my gun, avoiding the first blast
barely. I recall it shredding some of my hair off.

By the time I grabbed my gun and was
recovering from my roll, I had already heard the
shot gun cock and I knew he was already getting
ready to fire a second time! I looked up, and he
was just squeezing the trigger! Normally, a shot

gun blast against ballistic armor like my leather jacket wouldn't do too much but knock you over. However, I took my jacket off, and most of my mid-section was exposed now since I tore up my shirt to bandage Crystal's arm. I knew I was a goner, but something inside me was propelling me to stand. The next blast went off and, amazingly, most of the spray hit my cyber arm as I was pulling it up. Didn't even phase it! Some of the pellets sank into the soft flesh of my stomach and my left leg. But the adrenaline was already pumping. All I could do was aim and FIRE! The first two rounds knocked him back. That should have been enough, but I didn't stop. I started walking toward him, firing rapidly.

Somewhere, something, deep inside of me, snapped! I just kept shooting him! I followed his body into the office and I didn't stop shooting his body until the clip ran dry. Then, slowly, bloody, and suddenly very fatigued, I emerged from that office. The look on my face must have been bad, because Crystal seemed a lot whiter than usual, and Charlie looked like she had just seen a monster. Crystal watched me as I slowly walked out. I was trembling, I could feel it. The chamber of my Desert Eagle was open and bare and it and the barrel were hot and smoking. That clip had 15 shots in it. It was full before I fired it. I emptied 15 bullets into a man without even blinking. Slowly, almost mechanically, I walked over to Charlie and Crystal, both now standing. When I got directly in front of her, the grip on my gun released and it dropped to the floor beside me. I hardly noticed. I was still looking at her blankly.

"....he's dead...." Was all I could muster.
Crystal's face seemed pained. Like a mother who
just watched her child go through a terrible event.
Slowly she reached her arms out and pulled me
against her, my head resting on her bust.
"...now you finally know what it's like." She said,
as she held me. My mind was still a blur. I didn't
even know what she was talking about.
"What WHAT is like...?" I asked in a distant, far-
off voice. She ran her fingers through my hair as
she had done many times before, the end of
Charlie's story echoing in my mind.

"I want to get them back for what they did to my
family. Even if it's only a little bit. I know it will
never bring my family back. But at least maybe
my father can rest in peace..." Crystal stroked my
hair lightly then replied blankly to my question.
"To kill someone without remorse. You're now a
runner. Your innocence...is lost.".......
"Maybe my father can rest in peace...." The
words echoed through my mind. How could this
solve anything...? Much less bring anyone any
kind....of peace? I still don't know.

Chapter 7
Frantic!

August 30th 2061

Redmond Barrens District, The Rat's Nest,
21:30:09pm

It had been over a year since that night at
Boeing. The events of that night were now, more
just like distant images. But the pain, the feeling,
the darkness, was still quite real. I don't think I
ever truly recovered from that night. Even to this
day, I'm different than I was before that. I guess
truly my innocence was lost. However, life
moved on. And so did I have to. A few weeks
after that night Crystal and I had heard of a new
Johnson that frequented the Rat's Nest. A small
pub in the Redmond Barrens, about 2 miles away
from our apartment. Yes I said OUR. Crystal,
Charlie, and myself decided things were best if we
all lived together. I didn't give a shit, my
apartment was pretty much empty accept for my
bed, a couch, a chair, and the kitchen table. It was
a decent sized apartment. Big enough for the 3 of
us.

We had begun taking runs from this new
Johnson. They weren't much at first. Body guard
duty. Yeah, baby-sitting. Talking to local gang
officials, and mule work. Didn't really pay the
bills but we were getting regular jobs. Then
slowly he began to trust us with more important
jobs. Instead of escorting some loser across the

sprawl, we started guarding shipments, packages and actual places of interest. Which brings us to the job we had to do on that night. I remember it clearly. I was sitting at the bar, the usual regulars that frequent that dive were in. A BTL addicted Elvin whore was working her tricks. She propositioned the three of us once. Said she really needed the cash. We, of course, said hell no! The Orc shaman wanna-be was at the other end of the bar. Doing cheap parlor tricks trying to find a sucker to pay him money to do simple illusions and kids magic. He had all of Charlie's attention the one night. He almost got her too!

He was making bouquets of roses appear out of thin air it seemed for her. She was about to pay him 200 creds just when Crystal showed her he had a bunch of novelty magic props up his sleeve. He was so pissed with us that evening. Though we got a good laugh out of the bar tender. Then there was that creepy guy that always dressed in all black in the booth near our Johnson. He was there every night. Same time, same place. Sometimes I swore he never left. I often wondered if the dude was even still alive. He never seemed to move and I could swear I never saw him breath. Always had the same drink. I never paid close enough attention to see if the liquor in his glass went down or not. To be honest, I just wanted to get the fuck away from the guy! The one thing I did notice about him

however, was he had a strange crest on his gloves.
A crescent moon and stars I believe it was. Odd.
Odd, and creepy at the same time considering it
was the same as the tattoo on my chest. And the
same as the crest on the handle of my Desert
Eagle. The crest on my gun, as well as, the tattoo
on my left breast were there when I woke up in
the hospital. It made this guy even more creepy
since I was praying to whatever higher power was
listening that we weren't related in any way!

I had just finished my beer. Really, that was
the only alcohol I drank other than Elvin Wine on
occasion. A little fancy and expensive for my
tastes and budget. But it sure did go down
smooth. Crystal was making her way over to me.
I let her do most of the talking when it came to
getting us runs and jobs. She was a much better
negotiator than I was. She was beginning to teach
me a thing or two about negotiations. Even
though I was now considered full-fledged runner,
I still knew I had a lot to learn. Though I'd never
admit it to her!
"How's the beer?" Crystal asked, in a socially
bland tone, as she sat down next to me at the bar,
a small holo-pix in her hand.
"Stale, warm, and watered down as usual." I
replied with the same socially bland tone as her
own. "What do you got for us?" I asked as
Charlie slid over a stool next to me.
"Well, Crystal began, it's definitely different." I
waited for her to finish.
"Mr. Johnson has asked us to meet with one of his

contacts. A Street Samurai by the name of Glock."

"Interesting name." I said, as I finished my beer, crumpling the now empty can into a ball of tin foil with my cyber arm.

"So, I continued, what kind of a job is it that we require "additional" muscle? We already got one Street Samurai, a Weapon Specialist and a Rigger. Wouldn't adding another Samurai be a waste of man power and money?" I questioned the purpose of meeting this contact as I watched the Elvin hooker proposition a local Orc ganger. The Rat's Nest was a predominately Orc hang out. So it was typical to see bar fights and an occasional gang tussle. Tonight, however, was a slow night. We had only seen one dwarf get his brain splattered across the bar walls, which had begun to take on a red tint. "The Johnson didn't say." Crystal explained,
"he said that the contact would explain in full when we met with him outside Stokers Coffin Inn." I groaned and rolled my eyes, sliding a cigarette from my pack up to my lips and lighting it. After a long drag and short exhale, I continued, smoke rolling from my pink lips as I spoke.

"So how much are we making for this job?" Charlie listened quietly while ordering herself and me another drink. Charlie and I had formed a love/hate bond over the year after that night at Boeing. Her childish innocence still irritated me, but I could deal with it in a small dose.

"Here you go Raven." Charlie said with eager kindness as our drinks arrived.

"Thanks Charlie-girl." I replied as I cracked open my beer and took a long drink. I was beginning to think that maybe even she looked up to me in some way. So I tried to be nice to her.

"1000 credits." Crystal replied to my question of payment in her typical flat tone.

"1000 creds? That's it?" I replied. I was rather unenthusiastic about the payment.

"Do we have to share the money with the Johnson's contact?" Charlie quietly asked. I shifted my eyes to her as I was downing my 5th beer of the evening. I was actually kind of surprised she even spoke. Typically, Charlie didn't ask many questions about our jobs. She just did them. And she usually didn't take part in mine and Crystals little disputes we have. So I had to give her the due attention.

"Yes, Charlie, Crystal replied, with a little more enthusiasm this time. Apparently Charlie's question had her interested as well.

"We have to split the payment with him."

"Oh great!" I complained ,rolling my eyes and raising my arms in disdain.

"As if we're not scrapping the bottom as it is. Now we gotta share our pay-out with some dude we don't even know? What the frag'n hell for?" I grumbled and complained some more ordering another beer to try and dull the irritation growing in my head.

"I have to agree with Raven Crystal." Charlie spoke up again, her voice still really small compared to what you'd expect to hear from a runner. In fact in most cases when we were at the bar we had to listen really carefully when she spoke, or we could barely tell she was talking over the sound of the juke box playing. Doing some quick math in her head, Charlie continued with only a brief pause;

"That will only leave us each with 250 credits. That's not much for all the work we have to do." I cut in with my own grievances.

"Yeah, couldn't you get us a better deal than that?! I thought you were the one with the negotiation skill? What the frag Crystal!?"

The beer wasn't helping to ease my irritation. In fact, I think it was only making it worse, considering it tasted like soy-wheat mixed with warm toilet water. Crystal's eye brow twitched and I think we were starting to give her a migraine. That and the fact that the Orc magician kept making stupid sounds when he did his crappy tricks.

"Look! She hissed, it's the best I could get! I just sat over there for an hour negotiating with the fat greasy slob for that! Unless one of you wants to offer YOURSELVES up for "collateral", and I think both of you know exactly what I mean by THAT, I suggest you two stop whining and be happy with what we got!" Crystal tossed us the holo-pix that had the picture of the Street Samurai we were meeting. "Besides, if you don't shut the fuck up, I'm going to take a huge cut from BOTH of you two's share for annoyance fees!" "Alright, alright!" I said, handing Crystal her rum and coke. "Gawd, shaddup! PMS much?" I looked over the holo-pix with Charlie. Trying to memorize the features of our contact. He was a tall man with a large build. Crew cut hair and a 1980's action flick Rambo-esk red head band on his head. Dark hair, dark eyes and typical stern look you'd expect from a chrome head.

There was, however, one major thing missing. Most street samurai have cyber ware. In fact, most times, it's hard to tell where their meat bodies end and the cyber ones begin. Crystal had a good bit of cyber ware as well. However, her cyber ware was mostly prosthetic. Hard to tell from the real thing. This guy had none. After taking a moment to examine the holo-pix well and get a good image in my head of what Glock looked like, I passed it back to Crystal. Finishing my beer, I slammed it down on the bar counter.
"Alright, I grumbled, throwing my leather over my shoulders. "Let's get this over with." I tossed a couple creds on the bar to cover our tab, and began walking out. As I passed that booth where the strange black clothed man always sat, I felt an eerie presence. Similar to what I felt in my dream. It caused me to stop a moment and look over toward him. And, for the first time, I saw the man turn to face me. And from the shadows I saw a green cyber eye light up. My blood ran cold. It was the exact same kind of eye I had seen in my nightmare. I didn't realize I had frozen in place for so long. I was staring at him for a long time. I

could swear he could see right through me with that eye. I felt a cold hand on my shoulder. I almost jumped out of my skin.

When I turned to look at the owner of the hand, I saw Crystal.
"Hey, are you alright Raven?" The feeling I had must have been showing because she looked concerned.
"Yeah I'm fine. Just got caught up in a thought there for a minute." I put my hand on Crystal's shoulder and smiled with an attempt to look cool and collected. Apparently it either didn't work, or she just wasn't buying it, because her concerned look didn't change much.
"Are you sure cause we were calling your name and you didn't respond. You just stood there. You aren't drunk already are you?" I watched her eyes move from me to the silhouette of the man I had been staring at. When I turned to look, he had gone back to the way he was before. Almost like he never even moved. I felt a cold chill run up my spine, but I shook it off and turned my attention back to Crystal. "Yeah I'm cool. Let's get going." We left the bar and I didn't look back. But I couldn't shake the feeling that that man was the man from my nightmare. I had to ask myself, was it really just a dream after all? Was something warning me about something horrible yet to come? Or was I just losing my mind?

Redmond Barrrens District, Stokers Coffin Inn, 22:00:45pm

We decided to walk from the bar since the Inn was only a few miles away. Crystal left her car in the care of Charlie, who was rigged into it and waiting if we needed her. Charlie had a VCM installed in her. No, not a video cassette recorder like they used to have back in the day. VCM means Vehicle Control Module. Some people just call them "riggers". A rigger can jack their brain directly into a car, plane, boat, even drones and other such machines that come equipped with a rig-point. After Charlie's upgrade on our cars, she added rig-points to both cars, just in case we needed her to come in and pick us up. She may not have been very tough, or even very good at shooting, but to see the girl drive, WOW! It was an impressive site. Guess you spend enough time working on machines, you might as well learn to operate them too.

As we rounded the corner, we noticed a man, standing under a street lamp, roughly matching the description of the man in the holo-pix. We stopped a moment to observe him. He was leaning against the lamp post, arms crossed, looking around. However his attention seemed to be focused mostly in our general direction. However, he seemed to be watching the road more than the side walk. Meaning he was expecting Crystal's car most likely, rather than us to be on foot. I cocked my head slightly, keeping my sights on him but still addressing Crystal.

"Hey, sis, that looks our guy down there." Crystal had about the same posture I did. She was keeping a close eye on him as well, but cocked her head slightly toward me.

"Yeah, I see him too. You notice what I notice there Rave?" I smirked slightly and nodded. "Yeah I do. He's looking more toward the road than to the side- walks and alleys." Crystal nodded.

"He was expecting our car, not us to be on foot." "Johnson must have told him some information about us." She added. I nodded, and whispered, "Wonder if he also knows there's three of us instead of two?" Crystal responded with a whisper.

"Only one way to really find out."

We began moving toward this contact in unison. Soon as we started to get close to him, he stood up and took a more attentive posture. We met him in the circle of light produced by the street lamp. We were all sizing each other up, there was never much trust in a first meeting. Never know when some-one is just waiting to shoot you in the back these days.

"You the guy?" Crystal asked, intentionally being as vague as possible. Though this guy matched our holo-pix description of our contact, we still had to be 100% sure.

"I was told there were three women. Not two." He responded in a flat tone, apparently he knew enough about our group to know that there were three of us. So far this was going about as well as any first meeting can go. Crystal relaxed her posture slightly, placing her hands on her full hips.

"And we were told that we were meeting a Street Samurai. I don't see no cyber ware on you." I looked at Crystal with a questioning glance, I wasn't sure what that had to do with anything, but I was letting her do the talking here.

The man shifted his hand toward the opening in his coat. I immediately drew my Desert Eagle and pointed it in his direction. Crystal drew her sword from her back and held it to his throat, as he produced two Wakasashi from under his coat and had one against Crystal's blade and the other at my neck, but my gun barrel was still in his face. I'd say this was a Mexican stand-off, accept that none of us were Mexican, at least to my knowledge, and we weren't in a church. The three of us stood there, glaring each other down. I have to admit, my trigger finger was getting itchy at that point. And if the guy wouldn't have said anything, I probably would have shot him on the spot. Looking back, maybe I should have.

"Mr. Johnson told me to expect three women, two by your descriptions, and a third smaller, younger woman. What happened to your team mate?" I kept my gun trained on him, keeping my big mouth shut. Crystal put her hand to her ear. "Bring it around Charlie-girl, everything checks out here!" Crystal's Viper pulled down the street and up to the corner.
Yeah, Crystal took my suggestion and we got some ear-bud radios. Good thing too, or a move like this wouldn't have been possible. As Charlie

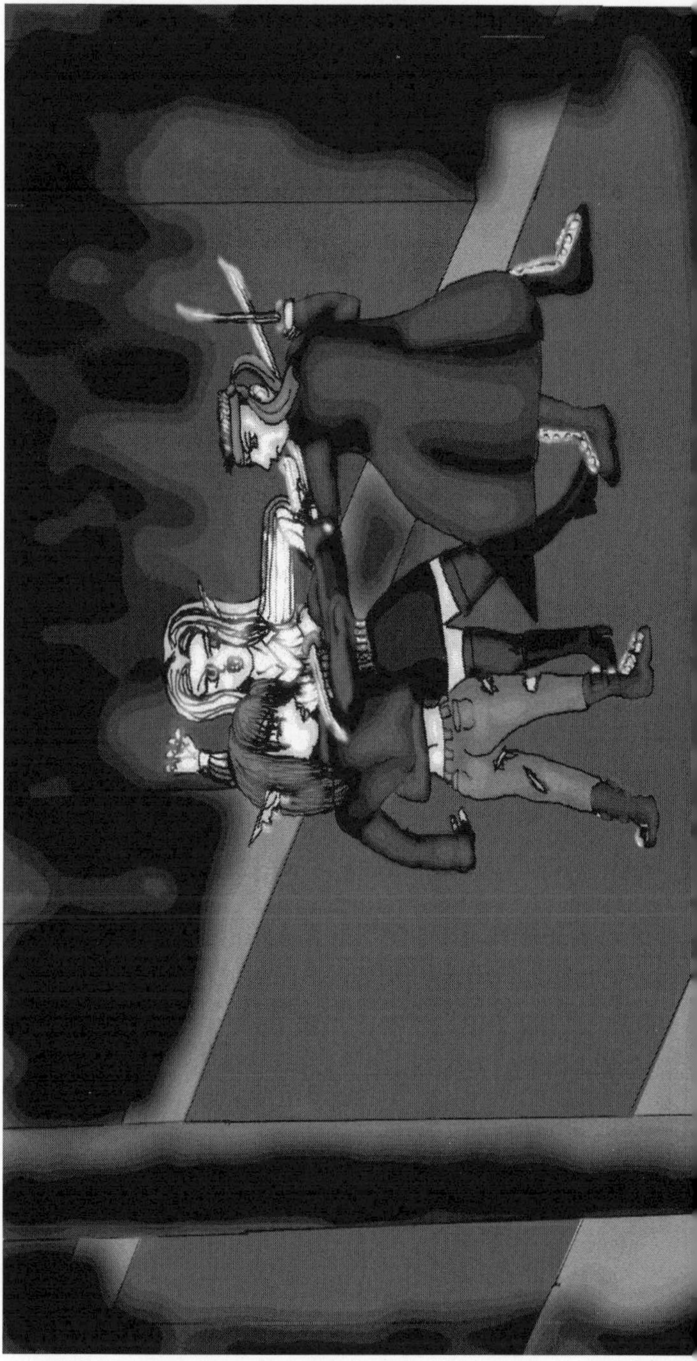

girl pulled up to the curb, she rolled down the
window.

"Did you get all that Charlie-girl?" Crystal asked
as I continued to keep my eye on the man in front
of us, gun still ready to fire.

"Yeah, I got it Crystal! So far, everything checks
out." Charlie smiled looking like she was all
important. The man looked between the three of
us then back at me and slowly relaxed the blades.
"Looks like the three of you know what you're
doing. I'm Glock, nice to meet the three of you.

I relaxed my gun, putting it back in my holster
under my jacket.

"Alright, now that that's outta the way. Can we
get on with all of this?" I crossed my arms over
my chest, lighting up another smoke.

"Johnson said you'd have further details on what
we're get'n into on this run. And why the hell we
need the extra muscle for this run. How about we
start talk'n about that?" 250 creds wasn't enough
for me to even really bother with. But we were
broke and I wanted to get this over with and get
back to finding a job that would actually pay.
Glock looked over at me and nodded.

"Agreed! But not here. Let's head out toward
Puyallup Barrens and I'll explain along the way."
I groaned, rolling my eyes, but before I had a
chance to protest this decision, Crystal respond.

"Alright, let's go!" Crystal moved over toward
her car, Charlie hopping out to let Crystal drive.
Glock got in the passenger side and I stopped.

"Hey! I complained, the hell am I suppos'ta sit?"

Crystal looked at me, then looked at the back seat where Charlie had already hopped in on the driver's side.

"In the back with Charlie. Why would you even ask such a dumb ass question like that for?" I grumbled, feeling the vein in my forehead beginning to pulse.

"Why the HELL am I stuck in the back seat!?" Once again, Crystal looked at me like I was retarded.

"Because the front seat is full and I'm driving. Is that beer starting to hit you late or something Raven?" I smacked myself in the face with the palm of my still flesh hand and shook my head. "….never mind!" I climbed into the back seat on the passenger side next to Charlie, who gave me the most sickeningly cute smile. I still didn't understand how one person could be that disgustingly sweet and innocent these days. I gave her a dull, uninterested expression and flicked my cigarette out the window. I was just getting ready to light another one when Crystal gave me that cold stare from her rear view mirror.

"You're not about to light up a cigarette in the back seat of my car are you?" I looked at her like she just asked me why I was breathing.

"Umm, yeah! What's your point?" Her glare only became colder and I felt that chill run up my spine.

"Don't even THINK about smoking in the back seat of MY Viper!"

I blinked at her,

"are you fucking serious!? C'mon! That's like asking me to give up eating or sleeping!" Her glare darkened.

"You wanna walk?" I raised my brow at her, "I'd rather walk and smoke than ride back here without cigarettes. Besides, this job's not worth the aggravation." Crystal quirked her brow at me.

"Fine, you go ahead and walk, but if you're not there in 30 minutes after we arrive, you're out." She stated plainly.

"WHAT!? I shouted back at her. Puyallup Barrens is at least 15 miles from here! I can't walk 15 miles in 30 minutes!"

Crystal yawned boredly at my protest. "Then it's either walk, smoke and go home with no money, or deal with it till we get there and bring home some cred. You're choice." I growled under my breath. Not only was I stuck in the back seat with Charlie like a damn child, but I couldn't even smoke. This was already shaping up to be a shit night and it had only just started. "Fine! I pouted. Let's just go! Sooner we get there the sooner I can get outta this cramped ass back seat and get some nicotine in my system!" Crystal grinned mischieveiously as she started down the road.

"Now you kids behave back there!"

"Fuck you ya fucking bitch! If you were my mother I'd put MYSELF up for adoption! Whore!" I crossed my arms and leaned back in the seat, trying to get comfortable. Charlie looked over at me and added her two cents to the conversation.

"You shouldn't smoke anyway Raven. It's not good for you!" I turned my head toward her, I didn't have to say anything the look in my eyes must have told her I was about to beat the living crap out of her. But I said my piece anyway. "Shaddup Charlie!" She shrank back in her seat and went quiet.

"At least this can't get any worse." I had absolutely no idea, how wrong I was about to be proven. Things were about to get far far worse!

Chapter 8
Frantic! Pt 2

August 30th 2061
New Seattle

Puyallup Barrens District, 22:10:45pm

"The mission we're working on was kept so quiet because there were quite a number of chances for information on it to be leaked. That's why I was so cautious when I met you two." Glock was telling us more details about our job while we were driving. I listened in only because I had to make sure I knew what was going on for Crystal and Charlie. To me, this job wasn't worth the time or the effort for only 250 credits. But I still was going to make sure my team mates were safe.

"There's a small run-down apartment building out here. There's a small gang of thugs in there making Stim-EX and selling it on the streets. Crystal stepped in to interrupt,

"No offense if you have a thing against drugs er whatever but, that really doesn't sound like the problem of a runner crew. That's more police or vigilante work than runner work."

Glock nodded in agreement before he continued, "That's true, but do you guys even know what exactly Stim-EX is?" Crystal shook her head, I shrugged my shoulders and Charlie simply replied

"Uh uh." Glock continued from that point,

"Stim-EX is a powerful drug derived from the use

of Stim patches. They mix a cocktail of drugs in with the stim patch; usually PCP, Angel Dust, Heroine, or some other hard core, heavy drug that makes the people using these patches not only heal up quicker, but also go on a rampage. A human on one of these patches is as hard to take down as an enraged Troll. Imagine, what an Orc or Troll on these patches would be like?" I replied with a rather snide tone.

"Wow, so they developed a drug to make Orcs and Trolls even more pissed off and hard to kill than they already are. Score one for chemistry nerds everywhere! Still doesn't really explain why we're all here." Glock nodded again to concur with my response.

"Yes, under normal circumstances, this really doesn't mean shit to any of us. However, this particular group of thugs is cutting in on the profits and drug running territory of a very influential client. That particular client has contracted us to run them out of town. By any means necessary.

Crystal looked at me through the rear view and my eyes met the gaze of her cold blue pools. We both were thinking the same thing however, she was doing the talking as usual. "Okay, she began, that makes sense why they chose a runner crew to deal with it. They didn't wanna get their own hands dirty on this one. But why send an extra man in on the run? Raven and myself could handle a couple thugs trying to be big time drug runners.

"Amen to that sistah!" I replied smirking. Glock looked back at me with a questioning glance and I just glared at him, I knew he was questioning my talents cause I wasn't as "hardcore" looking as Crystal. I hated that shit!

"That might be true." I interrupted him there with an annoyed snap.

"It IS true! Don't question our ability buddy, when we haven't seen shit of yer skills yet! Just cause you had your pretty blades all out in our shit earlier, don't mean jack! IF I woulda wanted to shoot you, I wouldn't a waited pal! Trust me on that one!" I was more talking up my skills on that one, but I was trying to play it off as I was defending all our skills. Crystal picked it up and rolled her eyes at me in the rear view.

Glock looked over his shoulder at me, apparently he didn't appreciate that comment but he continued explaining regardless.

"You guys have me on this, because some of the thugs have been using the stuff, so their all messed up and crazy. The sober guys will be easy to take out IF your skills are what they say they are. However, the guys that have been sampling the product will be a completely different story. Luckily, from what information I've been given, there doesn't appear to be any Orc or Troll thugs in the building. So hopefully we won't have to deal with any enraged beasts. "So what your handing us here, I responded with the same snide tone as before, we're going into this place with only half assed Intel? That's great, just wonderful! This aint even worth it for what we're getting paid!" I grumbled, trying to stretch my legs out which were getting cramped but I couldn't. Crystal's car was nice and all, but it sucked for passenger space.

Crystal continued asking questions, just ignoring my foul mood.
"So, what else can you tell us? Any information on the lay-out of the building, number of guys inside, any security measures, type of weapons they'll be carrying? Anything along those lines? Glock shook his head.
"All I know is that there are 5 floors to the apartment complex. The main lab is housed on the top most floor. So every floor before that will have armed guards. I assume most of which will be carrying basic street level weapons. Automatics, shot guns, and Sub Machine guns. I sighed with disgust.
"Great! We don't even know what the fuck we're walking into here!? How the fuck they gonna send us on a mission like this without shit for info on it?! This fucking reeks of bullshit! Seriously!"
As soon as Crystal stopped her car, I got out the back, groaning and complaining as I stretched my legs and lit up a smoke. I almost hit Charlie in the face with the door as she was leaning over to ask me what was wrong. If I would have noticed, I might have apologized. But this run didn't sit right with me.

Crystal parked the car and jumped out.
"Charlie, keep an eye on the car!" She shouted back as she followed after me.
"Raven….RAVEN!" She shouted to me. I stopped and I must have had a pretty pissed off

look on my face, because she actually stopped a moment when I looked at her. I'd have chalked it up as an accomplishment, me scarring Crystal for a change, if I hadn't been thinking about other stuff. She came up to me and walked beside me a ways.

"You got an extra smoke?" She asked, trying just to be friendly right now. I handed her a cigarette without another word.

"Got a light?" She asked again. I felt my neck twitch it only did that when I was overly stressed. "Jesus fucking Christ sis! Need me to smoke it for you too!? Maybe kick-start your lungs while I'm at it?" I normally didn't get that lippy with Crystal. A: I knew, just like me, she didn't like being mouthed off to for no reason. And B: I really did like her. I cared a lot about her, maybe more than I should, and I respected her. But this was an extreme case. And I think Crystal picked that up too.

"What's bothering you Raven?" She asked as she stopped by an old abandoned building. I stopped as well, mostly because she did.
"What makes you think something's wrong?" I responded without even looking at her. She walked up to me, exhaling smoke slowly.
"Well, for starters, you've been more of a bitch than usual. And that's an accomplishment for you Rave." She gave me the biggest shit eating grin I've ever seen on her in my life.
"Ha Ha! Very funny sis." I let it just roll off me. She was right, I was being a mega bitch right now. But I had a really good reason for it.
"Second, I know that look in your eyes Raven.

You only get that look when something's bothering you. What's wrong? Ever since we started talking about this run, you've been acting odd. You know you can talk to me. So what's the prob?" I took a long drag on my smoke, trying to calm my nerves down slowly exhaling then looked up at Crystal, replacing the smoke to my lips.

"This run. Everything about it just feels wrong! We're only making 250 creds. TWO HUNDRED AND FIFTY SIS! That's shit compared to what something like this would usually bring in. Second, we got this guy who doesn't know jack about this run. All he really knows is that there's going to be resistance. He doesn't know how many guys there are, or really even their weapons."

"Well", Crystal started but I interrupted, I already knew what she was going to say. "Yeah, he gave us an "educated guess" on the weapons. And it wasn't very "educated". If I was going to be run'n an operation of this caliber, I'd have my guys with assault rifles, shot guns, and sub machine guns. Not just automatic pistols and SMG's. I'd want some major stopping power in case someone decided they were gonna grow a set and come through my door." Crystal nodded at me, but she still wasn't fully convinced. "Well ya know Raven, not everyone has the gun knowledge that you do. He's probably not entirely off. Even you said they probably have Subs. So he's probably not too far off ya know?" I shook my head at her, and continued. "Sis, c'mon! Think about it! You aint dumb! Just cause the guy was smart enough to know how to handle a meeting, doesn't mean this guy knows what the hell else he's doin. We're going into this blind and you know it! This pay is not worth the risk! I know we're gett'n low on funds, and that we're really try'n to impress this new Johnson but, c'mon sis. This aint worth the risk."

Crystal looked down at her cigarette and went quiet a moment. I looked at her for a long time. "And you know it don't you?" I said, catching the look of sadness in her face. She looked back up at me she had a look in her eyes like she had something to say but didn't know how to say it. "C'mon sis, I said, stepping in front of her looking at her eyes.
"What's up? Talk to me! Something's been up with you! We've been together for over a year now and you've always tried to make the best decisions for me and Charlie. You've always kept us safe and didn't take any dumb ass chances. Talk to me! Why the sudden change all of a sudden? What's going on with you?" Crystal looked at me again but didn't say anything she just gave me this look like she had made a mistake and felt bad for it. But didn't know how to admit that. I shook my head,
"It aint worth it Crystal. I'm out! And you should be too! C'mon! Let's get Charlie and tell this dude "Fuck this we're out!" I started to walk away when suddenly crystal grabbled my right hand with her hands and just held it.

I stopped and slowly turned, looking down at

her hands holding mine then back up to her face.
"Crystal what's…" I didn't get to finish my
statement. She pulled me back to her and held
onto me. I didn't know what the hell was going
on. I just knew my face was turning red, and my
legs were suddenly getting really wobbly as the
sudden heat between them was growing. I was
trying to come up with something to say when she
cupped the sides of my face and kissed me. At
that point, I lost hold of my cigarette that was
between my fingers of my cyber hand. My mind
went completely blank. I couldn't even remember
what I was so worried about, or even what the hell
I was doing. I just stayed there for what seemed
like hours. But I guess it was only a moment or
so. She leaned over to my ear and whispered in it
which made it burn and twitch just like my crotch.
"I promise, if you finish this with me…I'll MAKE
it worth your while!" Something in her voice and
words made my body quiver from head to toe. I
swear my eyes rolled into the back of my head,
and I suddenly felt very wet.

I tilted my head slightly, my nose touching hers.
"…alright, for you." I felt like I was fucking
indestructible at that point! Even though every
rational fiber of my being was telling me to back
out now while I still had the chance, I wanted to
do this for her. It had been over a year, and we
had grown closer and closer. But it never came
this far. I felt like I had just crossed a bridge that
I had no hope of going back over now. And a part
of me, mostly my lower parts, wanted this! She
hugged me tightly again, and this time, I wrapped
my arms around her and hugged her too. My
heart was racing, and my face was burning. But I

liked the feeling. I liked being held, and I liked being desired. It's not like the desire wasn't mutual. It had been for a while. I just was afraid to really follow it. But now, now I didn't care. She had done a lot for me, and I wanted to thank her. I didn't know any other way than this. I think it's what she had wanted for a long time.

We returned to where Charlie was watching the car, Glock was already outside waiting for us. He looked rather concerned, we had been gone awhile so I couldn't blame him for that one. "You guys alright? You were gone for a while there." Crystal looked to me, she was handing me the reigns on this run now. I looked back to Glock and nodded.
"Yeah, just had to settle some things amongst the two of us. I'm ready!" I went to the trunk of Crystal's car, popping it open, I pulled out a M-90 Shot gun. I loaded 7 shells into it and cocked it. "Since we're going to have multiple platforms with possible automatic weapon fire I'll go in first! Crystal, you come in after me to cover my back. Glock, support where needed!" They both nodded to me. Charlie looked up at me from the car.
"What do you need me to do Raven?" I looked down at her, Charlie hadn't really used her gun much even though I had upgraded it for her and showed her how to properly fire it. She usually just worked on our cars and did the driving.

"You keep watch down here. I know you're

not much of a fighter but, if you see anything weird or anyone snooping around, let us know through the radio. If worst comes to worst, don't think! Just pull the trigger!" I knew the hardest part of this job would be if she had to shoot someone. She was still pretty innocent and hadn't really pointed a gun at another living person before. But she had to pull her weight on these runs. Charlie nodded to me.

"Okay, I'll do my best Raven." I nodded giving her a light smile as I headed toward the door.

"Alright folks!" I said, as I lit up another smoke, pulling the shot gun up to chest level.

"Let's get this shit over with!" I looked back over my shoulder and grinned at Crystal.

"I just got informed of something far more important that needs my "attention". Crystal smiled and winked at me. Glock looked between the two of us. I wasn't sure if he got what we were talking about or not, but he didn't say anything if he did.

I approached the door, Crystal's position staggered slightly off to my right and Glock further back and to the left. I pressed myself against the door way and looked at them. They nodded to me and I lowered my head and ran through the door tumbling to the side. I looked around, but there was nothing, not even a guard at the main desk.

"What's up in there Rave?" Crystal's voice came through in my ear. "

"It's quiet. Too quiet!" I responded. I had just stood up and began to make my way back to the door when suddenly it bolted shut. I had just enough time to pull my hand back as a security laser grid activated over the door.

"What the fuck!?" I quickly dove back around the corner as I heard footsteps coming down the hall.

"What the hell just happened!?" Crystal's voice sounded frantic over the radio.

"I don't know! There must have been some kinda silent security alarm or something! I must have tripped it when I came in."

"Are you alright!?" I heard her voice again in my ear, still frantic.

"Yeah I dodged the laser grid on the door. But I hear footsteps!"

"Raven…*STATIC*…what's Sta*tic*.....ho………*STATIC*....." "God fucking damnit!" I cussed, pulling the radio from my ear. "I knew this had bad news written all over it! Fuck, looks like I'm on my own for now!" As the footsteps in the hall drew nearer, I steadied my breathing and concentrated, my long ears twitching. Trying to hear the number of men and if I could hear the weapons they were carrying. I listened carefully to the sound of their feet hitting the ground. "….three men…" I whispered to myself, focusing on the sounds of their movement. I couldn't really hear the clicking of shoulder straps or of any type of automatic weaponry. So I was guessing they were either unarmed, carrying melee weapons, or just toting pistols. I had already ruled out the first two, which left only one other option. Pistols!

Outside, Crystal turned to Glock in a panic. "Glock! Is there a net terminal nearby here!?" He looked around.

"Yeah, I'm pretty sure there's one around the corner here. Why?" He asked unsure of what to do from here.

"No time! Just show me where it's at!" Charlie, who had been watching the whole time from the car, looked out the window.

"Crystal! She shouted to her as Crystal was running toward the terminal, What do you want me to do!?" Crystal looked back to her and shouted into the ear piece,

"Just do as Raven asked! Stay there and keep watch! I'm going to try and get the security system down!" Charlie winced in pain at how loud Crystal was yelling into the ear piece, but she replied fearfully.

"O..okay Crystal! Please be careful!" Crystal bolted around the corner following Glock to the terminal. "What do you need me to do?" He looked over at her as she was taking position in front of the terminal. She looked up at him as she flung her deck around her to the front, pulling the jack cord out.

"Just keep an eye on me! I can't do shit when I'm jacked in!" He looked back at her getting very frantic himself.

"But what about Charlie and Raven? Are you sure it's okay to leave them on their own? Shouldn't I try to find another way in?" Crystal turned and looked at him once more. "Don't worry about them! They can take care of themselves! Just keep an eye on my body!" With that she jacked into the system and went quiet.

I turned the barrel of the shot gun out around the wall and fired twice, hoping that the spread of the shot gun blast would, if nothing else, make them take cover. It worked slightly better than I thought. One guy went down, while the other two began running around firing blindly. I waited for a few shots to hit the wall near me and then I dove out from behind the wall. I fired twice again, knocking another over. I tumbled to a kneeling position just as the other was raising his gun to fire. I was alone on this, so I was left with my own techniques to keep me alive. I threw myself backwards, flat onto my back as the first two shots were fired, zinging past me. I then spun my legs out and up like a V to get me onto my upper back, I felt the vibration from the two slugs hitting the floor nearby. I then used the strength of my legs, spinning them around to roll me onto my side and rolled behind the main desk, just as two more slugs hit the ground where my body was. I stayed down behind the desk waiting for him to run out of ammo.

Sure enough, the moron kept firing even though I was behind cover. As soon as I heard his gun slide lock back I hopped up, bending myself over the desk backwards, just to keep my head out of the main line of fire, and blasted two more shot gun blasts at him. It knocked him off his feet and

through one of the apartment doors. I dropped
back down behind the desk and reloaded the shot
gun. "I'm not taking any chances here!" I said to
myself, almost hoping someone would respond to
me over the radio. But all I heard was static
again. I checked what I had left for ammo for the
M-90. I had another full reload plus an extra
shell. "This aint gonna last long. Especially if I
run into one of those guys using those Stims
Glock talked about." I said to myself as I cocked
the shot gun again and listened. I couldn't hear
anyone coming, so I jumped over the desk counter
and started my way up the stairs.

Chapter 9
Frantic! Pt 3

August 31st 2061
New Seattle

Puyallup Barrens District, 00:10:15am

    Charlie sat there nervously in Crystal's Viper, looking at the .38 revolver that I had fixed up for her. An overwhelming sense of shame suddenly filled her tiny chest.
"What am I doing?" She asked herself, resting her chin on the steering wheel of the car, her big round glasses sliding down her nose slightly.
"Everyone is putting their lives on the line. And here I am sitting in the car, just waiting. Crystal is trying to get the security system down, Raven is fighting and possibly getting badly hurt. And I'm just sitting in the car. I can't let my team do all the work just because I'm afraid! I have to get in there and help them." She slid her glasses back up onto the bridge of her nose and looked over at the glowing laser grid on the main doorway and huffed.
"But how can I do that?" She looked around the building, slowly coasting down the road, till she spotted another building close by the apartment that I was in.
"Hmmm... Charlie thought to herself, that might just work!" She pulled the Viper into a dark alley and cut the lights and engine, making her way up

to the building who's main entrance was boarded up. Using her trusty wrench, she pried a board loose and wiggled her skinny body inside. She never even noticed the flashing lights of the local STAR patrol coming up the main road.

As I was making my way up the stairway with haste, I had just rounded the landing as the stairs curved their way up toward the second floor, when I saw a door swing open at the top of the steps. A man rounded the corner and cocked the bolt back on an Uzi. My eyes went wide. In this position, he had the advantage. He was firing down at me from an elevated position. I had no time to turn around, and running back would only leave me wide open to his fire. So I did probably the stupidest thing in the world! I ran right at him! When he lifted the gun to fire I dropped straight down onto the stairs stomach first. My chest hit the step above me and my stomach hit the step right below it. I let out a loud "OOF!" As I heard the gun start firing. Bullets tore into the wall and cheap wooden railings, sending plaster dust and shards of wood flying all over the place and all over me. I felt a couple of the bullets zing past the tips of my ears and rustle my hair. I felt what seemed like someone cracked me multiple times right in the middle of my back with a whip or something. I knew he had hit me square in the middle of my back. Thankfully, this time, I had my coat on or I'd have been fragged.

I fired from my prone position on the steps, the

first shot blew his leg out from under him. In fact it took it clean off. He started to fall forward down the steps, so I fired again, just to make sure. This one caught him right in the face! His head splattered all across the walls, some of the fragments spattered across my face and in my hair. As disgusting as that was, it was the least of my concerns. I got up, rubbing my stomach and bosom.

"That's gonna leave a massive bruise!" I groaned slightly and started moving again. I no sooner got up to the top of the steps, when three more men stepped out of the rooms and started firing with assault rifles. I didn't even take the time to figure out what kind of assault rifle they were. I dove into the room the first guy came out of. I hit the ground and felt a searing pain go up my side. When I looked down, there was already a small trail of blood running down my side and soaking into my pants. I moved my coat to the side, and saw that one of the rounds pierced right through one of the softer spots in the armored lining of my coat and sank into my side. Luckily, it lost most of its velocity breaking through the armor of my coat but it still was imbedded in my side, and I suddenly felt a sharp pain coming from my ribs.

"Fuck!" I cussed, gritting my teeth. "The bullet must have cracked my rib! God damn it! I knew there'd be more than jus fucking subs and automatics! I heard the men stop firing a moment and begin to move down the hall. I tried to breath as easy as possible with my cracked rib and bleeding side. I waited and leaned around the wall and cocked off 3 more shots. I knew I hit the one pretty good, but the other two just rolled around the wall as the one I hit let out this psychotic yell and started unloading at me. I barely got my head around the corner. I felt a sting in my cheek, as a bullet tore through the wall by my head and the sticky wetness of something running down my cheek.

"FUCK ME!" I cussed again,

"This cock sucker's Stimming!" I saw then, what Glock meant by being as tough as a Troll to take down. I put my hand to my ear, ducking my head as another bullet zipped through my hair,

"Tell me you guys got something to tell me out there!? GUYS!?" Nothing but static again.

"You've got to be fucking kidding me!" I cocked the shot gun again and got up to my feet in a crouching position wincing more as blood began to drip down off my hip into a small puddle on the floor.

Glock looked around as Crystal was working in the system. He began to hear the sirens coming up the road.

"Ah shit!" He put his hand on Crystal's shoulder and shook her a bit.

"Hey! Crystal!" He shouted in her ear, shaking her a little harder,

"Crystal! C'mon we gotta get the hell outta here! It's STAR!" Crystal didn't respond because she couldn't hear him. She was deep in the system trying to shut down security. He didn't have the first clue about how a decker worked.

"Damnit! Charlie! Charlie where are you?" Static was his only response. Charlie was making her way up the stairs of the other building. The building had old faulty wiring, so it was interfering with the transmission. She had spotted a fire escape on about the third floor of the apartment building I was currently in. She noticed that the buildings were pretty close together, so she might be able to jump from one of the windows in the other building to the fire escape on the building I was in and work her way up to me. She was pretty brave for a sissy. Stupid, but brave.

Glock lost his composure. He couldn't get Crystal's attention while in the net, and he couldn't reach Charlie or me. So he did what any rational human being would have done. He ran! Problem was, he left Crystal all alone and unguarded! I had no idea what was going on. I had just moved to look out the door way when I go blasted in the face by the butt of this psycho's assault rifle. It broke my nose and bloodied my mouth. It caused my head arc backward, the pull of the muscles in my upper body sent a searing pain from my wounds through my body, and my legs gave out as I fell backward onto my back. I yelped in pain, looking up at the guy who looked more like a rabid beast than a man. He pointed the gun at me getting ready to fire. I pulled the shot gun up and fired, it blew part of his left hand clean off and he just screamed like a mad man and kicked the gun out of my hands before I could even cock the thing and fire again. It flew out of my hands off somewhere into the bullet ridden room and he stomped down onto my stomach with all the force that only sheer rage and madness could bring a person. I exhaled sharply and puked a combo of blood and what little bit of food I had in my stomach. I gagged and wheezed trying desperately to refill my lungs. He reached down with his bloody stump of a hand and his last good one and yanked me up to my feet by my hair.

I cried out in pain, only to be quickly silenced, as he socked me right across the cheek bone. He latched a hold of the front of my shirt, I tried to struggle away, but I was still dazed and he was moving way too fast for me to keep up with. In the struggle my shirt got torn to shreds, luckily I had a bra on, or the creep would have gotten a free show. He grabbed me by my arms and whipped me into the wall, my face smashed against the wall, further bloodying my nose, and causing my eyes to tear up. He struck me multiple times in my wounded side then grabbed me by my hair again and whipped me across the room over an old couch. I wasn't quite sure at this point whether he was trying to rape me or kill me. I don't think he really knew what the fuck he was doing either. All I knew is, I was lucky my ear was against the floor, or I probably would have never heard the other two guys entering the room.

Charlie found her way to the 4th floor of the old condemned building. She entered one of the apartments, and made her way to the window that looked out toward the fire escape of the building I was in. She broke and pried the boards away from the broken out window and cleared what few shards of sharp glass that were left with her cyber hand. She looked out across and began to realize the distance between the two buildings was far greater than she had originally thought. She looked down and gulped hard, gripping the window frame, as she began to carefully ease her tiny form out onto the little ledge outside. Once she got her footing, she clung to the window seal as she positioned herself facing the fire escape. She shifted her body around a little and almost slipped off the edge, she quickly grabbed a hold of the window pane and clung there for dear life.

"Okay...okay...Okay Charlie girl. You gotta be brave here!" She could hear the sound of gun fire even from this distance outside the building, so she knew something major was going down. She repositioned herself, and built up all the courage she had in her body.
"Alright! I can do this! Yeah! I can do this!" Steeling her resolve, she leapt toward the fire escape, but she misjudged the distance. Her tiny chest smacked right into the railing of it with a loud KLANG sound and she tumbled down.
"AH SHIT!" She reached out and caught the ladder of the fire escape with her cyber hand, dangling there a moment. "Wow! That hurt a lot!" She looked up then, suddenly, she heard a loud metallic groan. Like the metal of the fire escape was about to give. "Are you freak'n kidding me!?" Suddenly the ladder shifted and began to slide down rapidly. She screamed like a scarred little girl and grabbed onto the ladder with her other hand for dear life, curling her body up

against it.

"AAAIIIEEEE!!!" All of a sudden the ladder caught, with a jar, causing her to slip slightly and just dangle there by her hand. She was still a substantial distance off the ground. Her little body was shaking all over and she sweating profusely.

The other two men who entered the room were trying to calm their partner down to little avail. He was jacked up on stim and so many other chemicals, along with the amount of blood he'd lost from losing half a hand, he probably didn't even know where the hell he was anymore. Every part of my body was in pain and felt like it was on fire. Between the effect Crystal had on my crotch, the severe beating I just took, and the now broken ribs and bullet wound I had, it was a chore to move anything. But I kept thinking on what Crystal said to me.

"I'll MAKE it worth your while!" That thought made my crotch burn and tingle. I went with that! I slowly pulled the Desert Eagle out from my holster under my jacket and painfully, moved my body around, so that I was on my back, my legs were bent upward and my feet were planted, firmly, against the couch I tumbled over. I waited till they had calmed the guy down as much as possible and were making their way toward where I had fallen.

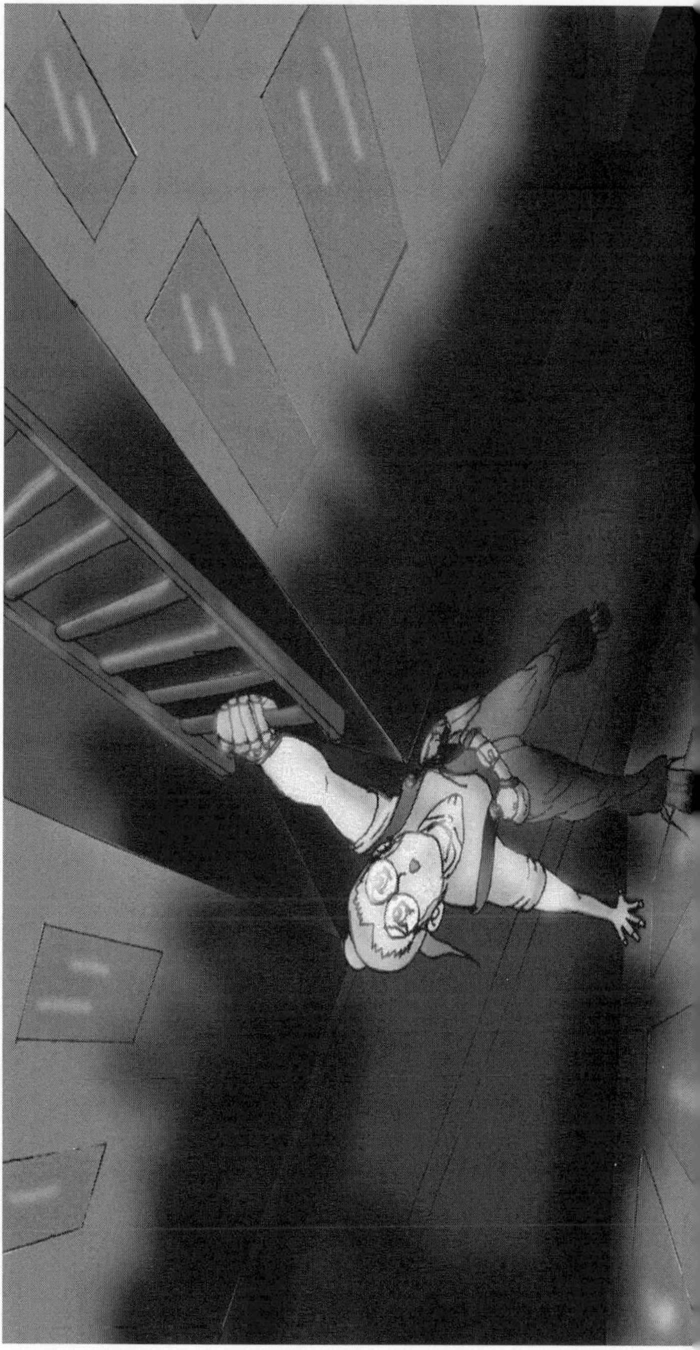

I cocked the slide back on my gun, the men heard it, as I figured they would. They started to pull up their guns and I used all the strength I had in my legs to push kick the couch, with both feet toward them. It skid across the ground and knocked their legs out from under them, their guns went off and I used the chaos of the gun fire to lift myself up to my knees and started shooting. I shot both of the guys that were making their way toward me dead. Unfortunately, the psycho path was still alive! *"This guy just doesn't wanna give it up!"* I thought to myself, as he came charging at me. I knew I couldn't handle another beating like the one I just took. And I really didn't want to be beaten, raped, and possibly eaten, god only knew what this guy had running through his brain right now. I threw myself onto my back again, pointing the gun up and lifted my feet up into the air so that the bottom of my feet were facing up flat. When he lunged at me, I caught his weight on my feet and just started firing almost point blank into his chest as I heaved his weight back and threw him through the window of the apartment off of my feet. He fell face first into the ground with a sickening splat sound.

I breathed a painful, heavy, sigh of relief and dropped the clip from my gun and put a fresh one in, cocking the slide back to load one into the chamber. That clip may not of been empty, but after that event, I wanted to be damn sure I had all

15 rounds to work with! I poked my head out of the door way and looked around the hallway, it seemed pretty clear, so I slowly began to work my way down the hall way, checking the other rooms for anybody that could be possibly waiting to spring out and jump me. As I made my way toward the end of the hall, I heard something coming from one of the other rooms. It sounded like movement. I wasn't taking any chances after the beating I just took, so I crept up to room slowly. The closer I got, I could definitely tell someone was in there. I could hear them shuffling around doing something. I wasn't sure what, so I slowly turned the knob of the door and pushed it slightly. I didn't hear any guns clicking and the door didn't become a piece of Swiss cheese. I quickly spun around the door and pointed my gun toward the source of the noise and yelled.

"DON'T FUCKING MOVE!"

Charlie dangled from the ladder for a moment before she felt she wasn't going to fall any further. She then slowly began to climb her tiny body up its length. When she started to get close to the top, she felt it shift sharply and groan loudly again.

"Ah crap!" She hurriedly scrambled up the ladder, just in time for it to fall with a loud crash to the alley way below. She panted heavily, thanking her lucky stars that she made it in time. But she didn't even have a moment of peace before she heard a man's voice say:

"Hey!? Didju hear that?!"

"Oh damnit ~~damnit damnit!~~" She cussed to herself as she clamored quickly up the steps, passing a window, as a man stuck his head out.

"HEY! Get back here ya little bitch!" Charlie squealed and went running up the metal steps of the fire escape.

"AH Shit! ~~Shhit shit shit shit on a shit~~ shingle!" The man climbed out and started running up the steps after her, firing a few shots from his assault rifle at her.

"AAAGGH!" Charlie screamed as she took cover behind some of the metal steps then quickly dove into a window. The man followed quickly after her.

"Now I gottcha ya little slut!" He poked the gun through the window and fired a few rounds then stuck his head in.

As soon as his head poked through the window, Charlie clocked him with all her might, right on the top of his head with her wrench. It made a loud BONG sound and the man's head hit the floor and then he fell back out the window knocked cold with a stiff concussion. She breathed a heavy sigh of relief.

"Phew! That was really close!" She no sooner got done sighing in relief, when she heard the toilet flush. Her face went pale as she slowly turned toward the bathroom just in time to see a man walking out of the bathroom zipping up his fly.

"Hey! What the fuck!? How the hell'd you get in here!?" The man didn't even wait for a response as he pulled his Uzi around to fire.

"EEEEEK!" Charlie shrieked and, out of pure instinct, whipped the heavy wrench she carried at the man. It socked him right between the eyes, making another loud high pitch BONG sound. The man's head flew back, the heavy metal wrench breaking the bridge of his nose, his arms flew out and the gun went off, ricocheting around the room. Charlie covered herself but not a single bullet hit her. They hit everywhere around her, but somehow, she managed to remain unharmed. She blinked looking around and chirped,
"Oh! Cool!" She ran over and retrieved the wrench from the fallen man looking down at his face which was dented inward in the shape of a wrench.
"JERK!" She stuck her tongue out at him and ran out the door way of the apartment into the main hall.

I pointed my gun down at what I thought was some more thugs but instead, it was a gang member on top of an Elvin whore. And not just any Elvin whore, the same one from the damn bar! The guy jumped up to his feet and raised his hands above his head, his junk all waving and saluting me. The whore, who we came to just call Trix, was hand cuffed to the posts of the bed, topless, the lower part of her body still covered by a dingy white sheet, thankfully!
"Ah for the love of fucking god!" I almost puked again, spitting at the sight that I saw.
"Get the fuck outta here!" The guy went running toward the door yelling at me.
"You're fuk'n dead bitch! My bois is gonna fuck yo shit up! Just you wait n see! Just you wai…"

As he was running toward the door, I stuck my foot out and he tripped right over it, as he was going down I brought the elbow of my cyber arm up right into his teeth and nose. I felt his nose break and his teeth shatter. He fell straight over backwards onto his back out cold.

"Who's gonna fuck who's shit up now bitch?" I taunted his unconscious body then I rolled my eyes, and looked over at Trix.

"Seriously Trix, what the fuck!?" She looked at me and pressed her chest out to me and rolled her hips a bit, trying to be all sexy for me. To tell the truth, it nearly made me gag.

It wasn't that Trix wasn't attractive. Hell no, she was frigging beautiful! She had this long blonde hair that came down in waves, and it always seemed to fall around her body and frame her face and breasts just right. Her skin was tanned, fake, of course, but she had these sexy tan lines from the bikini she always wore. She had a very slender waist and round hips. Her tits were totally fake, but they were actually pretty nice for being fake. Big D's, which was large for an elf. I was kind of fond of the tattoo she had, it was a Raven, flying around her navel, which was adorned with a big jewel encrusted bar-bell. Like I said, it wasn't that she wasn't beautiful, I just knew she had been with so many different men and women and was into all kinds of drugs and BTL's that she probably had contracted quite a few STDs.

"I was in the mood for something kinky. And he was paying, BIG, to get some of this elf pussy!" She said with a sultry voice to me.

I gagged again! The way she talked was a total turn off too. Her voice was sensual and sexy, but the words she chose to use were just foul. Even for a whore. I shook my head, wiping dried blood from my face.

"You couldn't have picked a worse place to be right now! The shit has hit the fan! And this place is a fucking powder keg waiting to explode! Ya need to get yer slutty ass outta here! And NOW!" She looked at me with those eyes like she was ~~raping me~~ with her mind. Course it didn't help I was shirt less right now and my pants were all torn up. She wiggled and rolled her body in that sexual way again and tugged gently on the cuffs which were holding her hands and arms back.

"MMM…are you sure you wouldn't rather finish what he started? I'm soo fucking wet right now! And I'd love to stick my head between those tits of yours while you finger ~~fucked~~ the shit outta me!" Once again, if I would have had anything left in my stomach to expel, it would have evacuated for sure on that one.

"Oh my ~~fucking~~ GAWD Trix! Will you just shut the fuck up and get the ~~fuck~~ outta here already!?" Besides, in my mind, I already had something a far hell of a lot better waiting for me once I got out of this shit hole.

She moaned softly and purred, tugging again at the cuffs. I swear me yelling at her only turned her on more.

"Well sweetie, suit yourself, but I kinda can't get out. I'm kinda cuffed to the bed right now." I watched the sheet move slightly, revealing her one leg and part of her rather beat up vagina as she spread her legs apart for me. I turned my head and yelled at her,

"~~Fucking A Jesus H fucking Christ~~ Trix, put it away! I don't wanna see that shit!" I turned my head slightly trying to use my hand and the size of my gun to block out her crotch but still make some form of semi eye contact with her.

"Look, I'll get you out of those cuffs but you gotta get the hell up outta here! Where's the key at?" I asked her. She finally shut her legs enough so that all I had to see was the little strip of blonde hair leading down to her clitoris which was, thankfully, covered by the sheet. That I could handle. "I dunno pet. I was pretty fucked up when he cuffed me. So I didn't see where he put the key." "You've got to be fucking kidding me!?" I sighed, and made my way over to her, she moved her leg and stroked my leg from the knee up to my crotch, she tried to press her foot up between my legs but I batted her foot away. "Will you stop that shit! Seriously! Don't make me beat the crap outta you!"

She moaned at me again purring louder, apparently threatening her was only turning her on more too.

"Mmmmm…Baby don't say that unless you mean it! My pussy's already soaking wet as is. That's just making it worse!" I so wanted to hit her. But she was all fucked up on drugs and after all, this was kind of her job.

"Oh my god shut the fuck up! And watch your face!" I pointed my gun at the chain connecting the cuffs together. She moved her head to the side and I pulled the trigger. There was a loud KAPINK sound as the bullet broke the metal links of the cuffs. I moved over to the other one that was holding her other wrist and did the same, breaking the chains loose. She pulled her arms down and rubbed her wrists slightly. Suddenly she reached out and yanked me down on top of her on the bed. I had about had all I could stand of this shit now and I literally shoved my gun barrel into side of her cheek.

"Look Trix! I've been nice about this up to this point! But so fucking help you god, if you put your hands on me one more time, I WILL FUCKING KILL YOU!"

She put her hand on the gun and slid it to the side slightly.

"You aint looking too good Raven. Let me help you." She seemed a little less sluttish and a little more serious. I figured she must have been coming down some off her high. But still, I didn't trust her this close to me.

"No thanks Trix! I don't want any of what you're selling. Physical or chemical! Just get the hell outta here!" She shook her head at me.

"You three were the only ones who ever treated me like a person rather than just a whore. You're not going to make it much longer in the shape you're in. I have some medical training. I wasn't always just a whore. Let me at least take that bullet out of your side and wrap your ribs for you. They look like they're broken. If you hit them the wrong way they could fracture further and puncture your lungs." I just looked at her, at first I thought she was just playing a game to get me to take my coat off so she could get her hands on my tits. Then I noticed that she had a look of shame in her eyes. "…you seriously know something about medicine and first aid?" I asked relaxing my gun a bit. She nodded to me.

"I was a medical assistant for a small doctor's office before Shiawase Pharmaceuticals took it over. I was fired because I had a fling with one of the officials and I didn't fit their new "Corporate Image."

I couldn't believe it. She was just like the rest of us. Another victim of a Corporate war. We were all the fallout from their wars. I sat up painfully on the bed and took off my jacket for her.

"Alright, but so help me if you do anything weird to me, I'll break your fucking arms off!"

Chapter 10

Miserei Mei

August 31st 2061
New Seattle

Puyallup Barrens District, 02:45:43AM

It took about an hour, but Trix managed to get me patched up. She pulled the shell out of my right side. I was lucky that it lost most of its momentum going through my coat. It was lodged right between my ribs. If it had gone any further, it could have pierced straight through my lung. My ribs were pretty badly busted up. On the right side, where the bullet hit me, they were cracked in three places. Not severely, but they weren't going to be able to take much more abuse without breaking on me. My left side, where I took most of the beating from the STIM-X addict were broken and bruised pretty badly. However they hadn't fully fractured, so as long as no one kicked me in the ribs again, I should be okay.

I had to admit she did a good job and, now that the adrenaline had worn off, I was starting to seriously feel the pain. She bandaged my ribs up really good for me and got the bullet wound patched up so it wasn't bleeding out anymore. However, it was the best she could do with the limited first aid supplies available to her. I slid my coat back on over my fresh bandages and, when the weight of the plates pressed against my shoulders, I groaned a little. My ribs were really tender and moving was a chore. I honestly wasn't sure if I was going to be able to make it any further. "Here." Trix handed me a three Stim patches she had sitting near her on one of the night stands near the bed.

"No thanks!" I said, shaking my head.

"I maybe in bad shape, but I aint desperate enough to take drugs and go all psycho like that crazy fuck down the hall. I like my mind to be in one piece."

Trix shook her head at me and held the patches out again.

"They're not the Stim-X patches. These are regular Stim patches. You're in a lot of pain Raven. I can see it on your face. If you're going to shut this place down, you're going to need these. They will give you boost. There's no way you'll make it otherwise." I looked at her face, even though she just patched me up, I knew she was a drug addict. So I wasn't sure I should trust anything she gave me. However, the look on her face seemed genuine, so I took them and stuck them into my coat pocket.

"Thanks Trix. I appreciate the help. I aint got a

lot on me right now, but I can float you a fifty for your work." She shook her head at me.

"You and your friends were the only ones that ever treated me like something more than a whore." She repeated what she had said to me earlier.

"I don't want your money. It's my thanks to you for just being real." I smiled lightly at her and tossed the 50 cred chip onto the bed regardless. "Get a real job Trix! You have a talent for medicine and there's a lot of sick and suffering people in this world. Why don't you try healing them, and you might find, you'll heal yourself in the process."

With those words of wisdom said, I made my way out of her room and started down the hall way. I was pretty sure by now that Crystal should have made progress on the security system. So the element of surprise should be back on my side. Which was good, as I was beginning to move up to the third floor, so I was right below the drug lab. I was going to need all the help I could get. Upon entering the stairway to go up to the third floor, I heard the door at the top of the steps open and the sound of footsteps coming down. I moved to dodge back down the stairs and winced in pain, almost falling down the steps. My ribs sent a sharp pain through my torso. *"Damn it! Looks like I aint got a choice!"* I heard the foot-steps round the first landing and start down

toward my location. I reached into my jacket
pocket and slapped one of the patches onto my
chest. Hurt a little bit as I quite literally
SLAPPED it onto my chest. Not the most gentle
way to apply a Stim patch to hurt ribs.

By about the time the medicine started to numb
the pain in my ribs, the footsteps were well within range. I spun around the side of the stairs and
shoved the barrel of my Desert Eagle into the face
of the person on their way down.
"End of the road for you Stim head! Hope you
got your fix for the day, cause the drug store just
closed for you junkie!" All I can say is, it's a
good think that I DON'T shoot first then ask
questions, or else I'd have shot Charlie right in the
side of her face. When the end of the barrel of my
gun hit her in the side of the head it knocked her
down onto the stair case and she actually tumbled
down and smacked her face off my knee.
"OH GOD OH GOD OH GOD! Don't kill me
don't kill me please!" My face fell slightly and
felt like I had a giant drop of sweat hovering
beside my head.
"I just wasted that bad ass line on YOU?! Damn
that's disappointing!"

Soon as Charlie heard my voice she looked up
at me from behind those huge glasses, the lenses
covered in plaster dust from bullets hitting the
walls around her. She dove at me latching onto
me around my waist, shaking like a leaf.
"OH THANK GOD ITS YOU RAVEN! " I
twitched my eyebrow, as even her tiny squeeze

hurt my ribs.

"I thought I was going to die! There were guns! And guys chasing me! And the fire escape broke! And I jumped across the alley and almost died! And I was so scared!" She squeezed me tighter, the pain forced me to bop her lightly on the top of the head with the handle of my Desert Eagle. She quickly released me and held the top of her head with both her hands.

"Ouchie!" She whimpered at me, with a disgustingly cute big eyed look, like she was going to start crying.

"What was that for!?" I groaned, with a combination of pain and disgust.

"Will you be careful! I'm not in the best shape!" I opened my coat to show her the bandages over my ribs and the Stim patch attached to my chest.

Charlie got all wide eyed again.

"Oh my god Raven what happened to you!? Are you okay!? You're not going to die are you!? Please don't die! Do you need a hospital!? Of course you need a hospital! You're all bandaged up! I need to get you to a hospital! But what hospital!? Oh God! Oh God!" My eyebrow began to twitch again with irritation. It wasn't that I didn't appreciate her concern, or that I didn't need help. I could probably use a good doctor right about now. Or at least a decent street surgeon. It was the fact that she was freaking out and I was still standing. So, I bopped her once

more over the head with the handle of my gun.
She shut up quickly and held her head again.
"OWWIE!!" She cried out, rubbing the top of her
head. "What was THAT one for!?" Once again,
she gave me the look like a child about to cry for
being scolded. I sighed heavily, my shoulders
slumping.

"Because you're freaking out! If I was
actually lying here on the floor bleeding out, how
much fekking good do you think you'd really do
me freaking out like that? NOW CALM THE
HELL DOWN!" I snapped at her. She shrank
back from me but she did calm down.
"Now, I continued, how did you get in here?
Weren't you supposed to be waiting with the
car?" She nodded to me.
"Well, everyone is always trying so hard to do
their best on these jobs. You and Crystal are
always getting into dangerous situations, getting
shot at, stabbed or hurt in some way. You two
took on all those mechanics for me at my old
garage during the Boeing job and never once did
you ask for anything from me for saving me. And
I barely even thanked the two of you!" Charlie
wiped her eyes, trying not to cry. "I lost my hand
because I was so afraid to fight back. I've always
been afraid and done nothing but cry, or just
tinker with machines."

I opened my mouth to speak but she just shook
her head,

"no! Let me finish please!" Couldn't argue with that. Besides, she made it this far on her own, might as well let her at least finish talking.

"I had you modify and upgrade my father's old gun so I could finally protect myself and avenge my family's death. But I haven't fired it even once! All I do is sit in the car and wait while you two do all the work and I just sit there." I could tell she was having trouble coming up with what she wanted to say.

"Look Charlie, don't worry about it. You do what you can by being our driver." She shook her head at me again.

"But I want to do more! What good does it do just being a driver when, if things keep up the way they are, I won't have anyone to drive?! I won't have anyone….at all." I guess it made sense why she was so upset. I thought that her waiting in the car was what she wanted. She wasn't very good in a fight and, looking at me and all my battle scars, who'd want to be in the type of fights you get into in this type of work? But she was right, regardless of all that.

"Alright, good enough!" I finally just gave in and agreed with her.

"But if you're gonna be in the heat of battle with me. You need to carry your own weight! Neither one of us are going to be any good to each other lying on the ground full'a holes!" Charlie nodded, wiping her eyes as we began to make our way up the stairs.

"And for the love of fuck Charlie-girl, stop frig'n crying! Runners don't cry!"

We made it to the top of the stairs and threw my back against the wall near the doorway, gritting my teeth as a searing pain went through the core of my torso from my ribs. Charlie looked over at me whispering.

"Doesn't it hurt to do that in your shape?" I let out a sharp

"*SHHH!*" In her direction as I leaned around to peak through the partially open door. She went quiet and just watched me. "*Of course it frigg'n hurts god damnit!*" I thought to myself. But I can't afford to be slowed down. I already had Charlie to worry about now, so I didn't have luxury worrying about myself right now or being gentle on my own body. There were two guys patrolling the hallway up and down. I could also smell a strong stench of ammonia, a common chemical used for cutting drugs. So I knew I had to be in the right place. The problem was how to do this without drawing the attention of every thug in the building? Would be easy enough to run out there and shoot the two guards. But that would draw everyone's attention. For me alone, moving from room to room dodging and shooting wouldn't be a problem. But I knew damn well there'd be no possible way Charlie could do it.

"Fuck!" I cussed quietly to myself. Apparently, I said it a little louder than I initially intended to, because Charlie looked over at me right after I said it.

"Not looking good?" Her voice was barely a whisper. I probably wouldn't have even heard her if I wasn't an elf.

"Yeah, it aint look'n good at all!" I responded lightly.

"There's two guards patrolling the length of the hall. And I can definitely smell ammonia so we must be on the floor with the labs. Problem with all that is, if I run out there and shoot those two guards, I'll get everyone's attention. Now for me, running, gunning, jumping and tumbling from room to room isn't a big deal. Even with busted up ribs I'm bet'n I'm ten times faster than these amateurs. However, you're not exactly the most nimble girl in the world there Charlie." Charlie looked down at the floor, holding her dad's revolver in both hands.

"I'm sorry I'm so useless Raven!" She sniffled like she was about to cry so I shot her a threatening glare.

"What did I say!?" She stiffened a bit and stood up straight.

"Runners don't cry! I'm sorry, I'm sorry!" She started apologizing repeatedly to me, so I glared at her again.

"And they don't apologize repeatedly for stupid shit either! Now shut up and help me think! We need to come up with a way to get past these guys WITHOUT drawing all their attention at once."

Charlie started looking around at the walls, the ceiling and the floor suddenly. It kind of reminded me of a child who was bored at the super market or store. I groaned and snidely responded;

"sorry that this is so boring! But you might want to pay attention little miss ADD, unless you find dying in a shoot-out more morbidly entertaining!

Just know you'll probably be the first to die. And a bullet to the stomach really fucking hurts!" Charlie gave me a pout face that made me roll my eyes.

"I am paying attention!" She replied sharply, in a way that reminded me of a young girl about to stamp her foot in a tantrum.

"Usually these old buildings have sprinkler systems, and I know you can't mix certain chemicals with water or else it messes them up. Like car oil. If you get water in car oil you have empty it all out and put new in. I raised my eyebrow at her.

"That's fascinating, really, Charlie but I don't see how that's supposed to help us in the here and now." Charlie looked over her shoulder at me as she was all stretched up reaching for something along the ceiling and stared at me for a moment. The look on her face made me believe she was wondering if I had any education what-so-ever. It irritated me.

"Either wipe that look off your face or I'm gonna knock it off your face! If you got a plan just frigg'n tell me! Don't look at me like I'm retarded!" She made a timid squeak sound and spoke, again, luckily I had good ears or I'd have never heard her.

"Well," she began, "if I can find a way to set off the sprinkler system, then not only will the water ruin all the chemicals they're using for the drugs, but everyone except for a couple guards will run out of the building thinking there's a fire or something." I looked at Charlie and blinked a few times.

"Alright I get the idea about the water ruining the chems and stuff, but what makes you think the lab nerds will just run away? It's not like there's actually a fire or anything." Charlie grinned mischievously at me;

"do you think that any of the lab "nerds" here are paid enough to wait around and find out if there is a REAL fire or not?" Something in her grin told me she had done something like this before. And I had to admit, she was pretty clever for being so useless in combat.

"Well aint you jus the lil trickster! Alright let's do this then."

After a few minutes of Charlie tinkering with some pipes and wiring, she looked over at me. "Hey Raven, do you still have some cigarettes?" I looked at her queerly;

"I got a couple, you aint picking up smok'n are you? Cause I really aint got enough for you to be bumm'n on this run." Charlie shook her head at me.

"No, no, I need you to light one up and blow the smoke up there!" She pointed to a small sensor in the ceiling. I looked up at it then back at her.

"Really? That seems a little too simplex to work. Are you sure?" She nodded swiftly.

"Yeah, I tweaked the wiring and increased the pressure of the water. Just a little bit of smoke from your cigarette will cause the system to gush water everywhere!" I nodded to her and pulled a smoke out of my pack and lit it. I took as deep a drag as I could with my ribs being sore, and blew the smoke up at the sensor and watched for a moment, but nothing happened. I let the filter of my smoke rest between my lips in the corner of my mouth and looked over at Charlie with a question glance.

"Sooo..where's all the water at?" She looked up at the sensor, which now had a small halo of smoke around it, then back to me.

"Maybe it doesn't work?" She whispered.

I was just getting ready to open my mouth and make a snide comment, when all of a sudden I heard the ear-splitting sound of a fire bell ringing and water started gushing out of the sprinkler system. I looked down at my cigarette which was now soaked and un-smoke-able then back to Charlie, spitting it out.

"Or maybe it does." It was all I could say as we were both now, soaking wet. We both leaned against the wall as the doors flung open, lab techs scrambling down the stairs. Luckily, we were safely hidden behind the doors. Once the small stampede was over, I looked back into the now partially flooded hallway and, sure enough, the guards were running back into the one room, trying to save as much product as possible. I smirked then looked over at Charlie.

"Alright, nice job there Charlie girl! Now, whatever you do, don't fall behind me! And shoot to kill!" I pulled the Berretta from the other holster under my coat, and started down the hall. I knew what I just said to Charlie wasn't going to be easy for her, but she wanted to be here beside me, so she was going to have to do her part. I made my way down the hall to the first room on the left side. Charlie's position staggered slightly behind me. I pressed my back to the wall, holding my guns up and slowly rolled around the door frame. We caught the guards completely by surprise! Soon as they looked up I shot both of them twice. They fell over dead into the pooling water turning it red.

Charlie stood there stunned a moment. It was the closest she had been to a gun fight since the events at her old Garage a year ago. Even then, on that night, she wasn't really there when I shot the fat mechanic. Right now she was standing right next to me staring down into the crimson water at two guys who had just been shot dead right in front of her. Her eyes were huge and her face was whiter than usual. As she looked up I lifted the Berretta and pointed it in her direction. She opened her mouth to scream but nothing came out. All she heard was the BANG of the gun and felt the blood spatter against the side of her face, as a thug fell not far behind her. I don't think she really knew what just happened. She just fell over onto her butt in the water and sat there. Wide eyed, teeth clenched tightly shut shaking. I moved over beside her and shook her a few times.

"Charlie...CHARLIE!" I screamed right into her ear and she finally looked at me like she was unsure of where she was. "Are you alright?" I asked her again. She nodded her head. "You gotta pull yourself together! I know this is intense for you, but you can't think of them as people right now. Think of them as paper targets. I'm sure you shot at paper targets before right?" She looked down at the dead man next to her.

"Paper…targets?" She repeated slowly. "I turned her head so she was looking at me and not the dead man. "Uh huh, yeah, paper targets. You know, at a shooting range? Those targets they have that you practice on? If think of them as paper targets, and not living people, it won't be so hard."

Charlie was looking into my eyes, trying to draw strength from me to do what she knew she had to do.

"It sounds so…heartless though." I kept a hold of her face and continued to talk to her.

"Do you think they see you as anything more than a target right now Charlie? They will KILL you without even thinking twice! You don't want to die do you?" Charlie shook her head.

"No, I don't wanna die!"

"Then you have to trust me on this!" I continued to look into her eyes as I spoke,

"don't see them as people. Just as paper targets! Don't think, just shoot!" She nodded lightly.

"I'll try my best Raven." I let go of her face and picked up my guns again.

"Just try your best!" I knocked over several of the tables, so what product they had, landed in the water and continued out into the hall. I barely got out into the hall before I had to jump back into the room to avoid gun fire. There were three thugs shooting from across the hall in the other rooms. I couldn't lean out far enough to get a clear shot so I was just leaning the gun out around the corner and shooting.

"Damnit! We're pinned down!"

I looked over to Charlie, who was still shaking like a leaf in the corner holding her gun. Bullets ripped through the walls and splintered the table and chairs, some of the drugs, that weren't soaked, started to ignite from the sparks of bullet ricochets.

"Are fucking kidding me!?" I growled in my throat, looking toward Charlie, who was huddled in the corner with her hands over her head. This was too much for her, and I knew it. I sighed and pulled another stim-patch from my jacket pocket. "Better to burn out then to be burnt I suppose." I said, quietly, as I removed the protective backing from it and slapped it onto my stomach. I knew this was more than I needed, but I needed the boost. I had to get the fuck out of here! And Charlie wasn't ready for this! I felt my heart rate begin to quicken, my muscles tensed, my hearing sharpened and my vision tunneled. Things seemed to begin to move slower. My common sense began to fragment and the only thing I could think of was killing every last one of this cock suckers. I lifted my two guns and dove into the hall way as bullets zipped by me, I swear I could almost see the tracers coming off of the bullet projectiles from their guns. I lifted the two guns and opened fire, everything seemed to be moving so slowly around me. I felt like I was actually in some form of bullet time. Did these stim-patches really contain this much stimulant? Or was I just this desperate? I didn't know, I couldn't tell. I fired twice from each gun. The first thug got hit with all four shots, I saw his body flail slowly, as blood began to spray from his wounds. He fell over backwards in slow motion.

As soon as my body touched the ground I rolled to my feet and threw myself against the wall, the two thugs were moving into the hall, as I was getting to a kneeling position. To me, they seemed to be moving like snails. I dove forward at them, rolling onto my back and sliding down the wet hall way on my back as I leveled the barrels of my Berretta and Desert Eagle at them and started firing as bullets flew past me. As I slid past them, I started to fire, I watched as my bullets ripped through them, two in the stomach of each of them, two in each shoulder, then one in each of their throats. As my slide slowed, I came up to my feet at the end of the hall, just in time to point both guns to the rooms on each side of the hall way and continue to fire until the clips of my two guns ran dry, dropping every gang member that came running my way. I slowly crossed the two guns over my chest and ejected the clips, I felt a strange over whelming sensation of blood lust building inside me, and a dark foreboding sense of joy at everything that had just transpired. I hated it! But, a deeper darker part of me, almost found a sensual joy in all of this. It was like my psyche was split directly in two, and currently fighting for control of my body. *"So, this must be what those stimed-out psychos feel."* I thought to myself as I reloaded my guns.

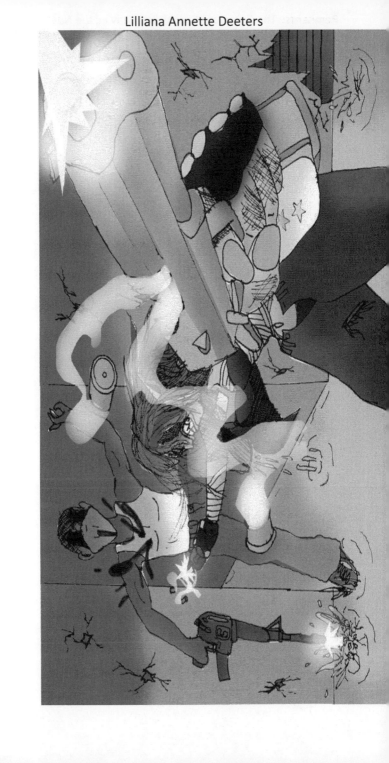

Charlie slowly made her way out into the hall she kept looking at me like she didn't recognize me. I could only imagine how I looked to her. Breathing heavily, hair dripping wet and hanging in my face, covered in blood and STIM-X resin, two smoking guns in each hand and a twisted grin on my face. I probably was more terrifying than the thugs were at this point.

"R..Raven?" She fearfully whispered to me. "Are you…are you okay?" I lifted my head my eyes meeting her own. My pupils had to be dilated, considering how much Stim was circulating through my blood right now. Not to mention how much of the drugs had probably soaked into some of my still open wounds. Even in my messed up state, I could tell by her eyes I looked like a mad woman.

"Yeah! I'm fine!" My voice had to be as twisted as my thoughts were right now. "Let's go!" I said darkly and quickly started making my way up the steps to the 5th and final floor, gunning down gang members as they came running down the stairs. As we reached the top of the stairs, a stimmed-out gang member ran head long into me, however, in my current state I was far more ferocious than he was. I smashed the side of his face with the elbow of my cyber arm, then followed through by shattering the rest of the side of his skull with the butt of my Desert Eagle. He flew into the wall and I dove on him smashing him into the cheap plaster-board wall with my knee. I heard the sound of his ribs snapping like twigs under the force of my knee and, to most people in their right mind-set, that would be a good instance to stop. I, unfortunately, was too far gone!

The sounds of bones breaking and snapping only threw my stimulant induced psychosis into a further blood-lust driven fervor! I began kicking this man, who was probably no more than 16 years old, further into the wall! Blood spattered against the wall and my face, but it only served to enhance my violence fetish. I reached in and drug the boy, who was already almost dead, from the wall and lifted him up with my cyber arm, holding him above me by his neck slowly choking the life out of him, laughing in complete delusional madness! I don't know what I was thinking, I don't even think I knew who I was or what I was even originally doing there. All I remember, is I felt something press against my right arm and I pointed my gun at it and turned my head. It was Charlie, clinging to my wrist, now, she had grabbed my arm with all the strength in her tiny body, I had almost knocked her down the steps backward when I pointed my gun into her face. I had even drawn blood, raking the barrel against her face and jamming it into her forehead. Even though she was too afraid to fire her gun at anyone, she was amazingly heroic to hold onto my wrist for dear life now, and shout at me. "RAVEN! Get it together! What the hell is wrong with you!? You're…you're acting like a crazy psycho! Please! Stop it! This isn't you! I know you're strong and I know you're capable of this but you have more self-control than this! Please stop!"

It was in that moment that my senses came back to me. I dropped the gang member, who tumbled down the steps in a bloody heap. He had ceased living a long time before Charlie brought me back. My legs started shaking and I could no longer hold myself up on them, I dropped down on my knees, my cyber arm gripping the railing with such urgency, that I actually made finger imprints on it. Charlie held onto my shoulders. "Raven! You don't look good! I need to get you out of here!" Just as she was going to help me down the stairs flames tore through the lower part of the wall. Even though the sprinkler system had been activated, the pipes had run out of water and the fire from the drugs was beginning to spread! "Oh crap!" Charlie exclaimed, quickly pulling me back up the stairs. "We're trapped up here! The lower floors are all a blaze!" I looked up weakly to the upper stairs.

"Keep going up!" I said. Charlie looked down at me as if I had completely lost my mind.

"Why would we want to go up!? If the building supports fail.." I didn't let her finish,

"Look! There's got to be roof access. In these old apartments, most of them had roof access through a small window at the end of the main hall. Its only five floors up, if we jump off, we should be okay. Unless you wanna try running through flames. I might make it, but with all that car oil on you, you'll go up like a torch!" She gave me a concerned look but nodded anyway. "Okay, are you sure you can make it?" I gave her as bold a grin as I could give her through the pain and weakness I was feeling. My over exertion had re-opened a few of my wounds and drained a lot of the adrenaline from my body. "Yeah, I'll be fine, c'mon! Let's get outta here!"

Though Charlie was apprehensive, she continued to guide me through the doors and down the hallway slowly. About halfway down, fires had begun to break out on the top floor as well, and we began to hear a strange rumbling sound as well as what sounded like something slamming against the wall of one the apartments on the upper floor that we were on ahead of us. "What the fuck is that now!?" I said, wincing at the pain in my ribs. Charlie continued to help me along.

"I dunno but we gotta keep moving! We're almost there!" Just as we were almost to the window at the end of the hallway, the wall of the apartment nearest the window burst outward, flames bursting into the hallway, causing them to quickly spread. Charlie fell over backward taking me with her as my body was in too much pain to support even her tiny weight,. Standing there, in the dust of plasterboard, smoke, and STIM-X was a huge stimmed-out troll carrying a sledge hammer and covered in STIM-X patches. As if a Troll ganger wasn't a big enough threat, one jacked up on psychotropic STIM-X and my body being busted up like it was made this far worse than it needed to be.

"You've got to be FUCKING KIDDING ME!?" I shouted, as the beast roared at us and swung the sledge around. All I could think of in that moment was if he hit Charlie with that thing, he'd crush every bone in her little body! I gathered what little strength I had left and threw her with my cyber arm down the hall. No sooner did she go flying, I felt a powerful blow hit me in the side. I felt my rips snap and crack under the force and blood squirted from the wound in my side, as the troll struck me strong right in my side. The massive force of the blow knocked me through the cheap masonry of the wall and into the burning apartment. My back hit the wall and I landed face down in the chemical dust and filth of the room.

I tried to pull myself up to my hands and knees but my stomach churned and I puked blood and I quickly fell back down onto the ground. "Damnit…I think that one hit broke every bone in my whole fucking body! I heard the troll's heavy feet coming into the room. Between the smoke, pain, and the massive concussion I now had, I couldn't really see him, just the silhouette of his figure coming toward me. *"Fucking son of a bitch! I gotta fucking get up! But I can't fucking move! Damnit! I can't move my fucking body! Move god damnit! MOVE!"* I remember shouting at myself in my head. But my body wasn't listening. The creature reached down with its huge hand and picking me up by my head and whipped me back into the hallway through the cheap wooden door. Even cheaply made, the door felt like it was made of oak when my body went through it. I hit the floor of the hall way and tumbled all over my self like a rag doll. What was left of the wall of the apartment, quickly collapsed down as the troll came walking through slowly. *"If this moron keeps this shit up he's going to bring the whole top of this building down on* ~~fucking~~ *top of us!"* My mind raced, trying to come up with something to get myself out of this one. But I couldn't move, so nothing I came up with was going to do me any good! As the troll approached me I ground my teeth together and growled weakly in my throat. I remember thinking to myself: *"Damnit, looks like this is it! I'm gonna die here! Sorry Crystal, looks like, I'm not gonna be able to keep our date…I don't have anything left in me to give. Guess you were wrong about me, I was just a wanna-be the whole time!"*

I glared up at the troll in defiance, I wanted to cry, I wanted to let all my grief out for being so pathetic, but I wasn't about to give this troglodyte son of a bitch the joy of seeing me cry. Then all of a sudden I heard it.

"RAVEN! YOU GOTTA GET UP!" It was Charlie screaming to me. The troll suddenly turned to face her and I felt my heart stop.

"Charlie you fucking idiot! Why the hell didn't you run away!?" It was the only thought that ran through my brain in that second as the troll turned to face her and began moving toward her. I don't know where I found the strength, but somehow I managed to pull myself up onto my hands as he made his way toward Charlie to scream, my voice straining.

"CHARLIE! GET THE FUCK OUTTA HERE! DON'T JUST SIT THERE! RUN!!!" It was no use, the poor girl was frozen in terror. Charlie was only 4 feet tall. I myself, was almost 2 feet taller than her. So this 9 foot tall troll was a titan in comparison to her. With some unknown strength, I managed to pull my Desert Eagle out of my holster and started shooting at the Troll. Several of my shots hit him square in the back, the shells made huge holes in his back and I could tell they blew straight out the front of him. After about 5 shots actually hitting him, he turned, his huge chest was a bloody mess of holes, several chunks of it missing and I could clearly see parts of his rib cage. He suddenly started running down the hall way toward me. I fired 2 more which got him in the legs, but he didn't go down.

"That's right you big cock sucker! Focus on me! I'm not fucking dead yet! SO FUCKING KILL ME YOU BIG NASTY TROGLODYTE ~~FUCK!~~" I shouted to him as he came running again, even with his legs all full of holes. I heard the loud ping-like click that my clip was empty, the slide of my gun locking back. A tired, content grin, fell on my lips as my vision started to blur and I slowly brought myself up to my feet, using the window seal to hold myself up with my cyber arm. *"That's right you big dumb son of a whore! Come to me! We'll both go to hell..TOGETHER!"* I braced my broken tired body for the impact of his huge form. Pressing myself back against the wall, so his weight would smash the window out. I had planned to let this big beast fall to its death with me. Then right as the huge thing was close to me I heard the sound a gun go off and the troll fell forward sliding in the water to my feet, a massive whole blown out of the back of his head. I looked up from the troll and saw Charlie, standing there, trembling, smoke slowly twirling from the barrel of her father's revolver. She had just shot and killed someone for the first time in her life.

I looked at her for a long time and then chuckled painfully,
"nice shot…Charlie girl!" My body slid down the wall and collapsed to the floor. Charlie came running over and placed her hands against me, which immediately became soaked in blood. Seeing her hands covered in my blood, and the lines of blood running down from the wound in my head, she started shaking more and freaking out.
"No no no no no no no nooooo! Don't you die! Not now! C'mon Raven open your eyes! Wake up! Don't die, please don't die!" Her hands were

shaking and flailing purposelessly, as fires erupted around her and pieces of the roofing were beginning to crash down around us. I finally parted my one eye looking up at her.

"…tell me…you didn't just save my life…for us to die in a burning building?" The look of relief on her face could only be compared to that of a person who just relieved themselves after almost pissing in their pants.

"Oh thank god! You're still alive!" ~~I snorted at her.~~

~~"God had nothing to fucking do with it! It was all you. Don't sell your accomplishments short by thanking dead deities.~~ And neither of us are gonna be alive much longer if you don't get us the fuck outta this burning death trap!" I couldn't move a muscle, my body felt like it had just been broken into multiple pieces. Even though, as far as I could tell, I was still in one piece.

Another chunk of the ceiling came crashing down near Charlie in flames. She quickly pulled my good arm over her shoulders and slowly brought me to my feet as best she could, pulling me out of the window, she pulled me up to the roof but our problems were far from over. In fact, the worst of our problems had just begun!

As Charlie got us to the roof, the sky was thick with black smoke and flames lapped at the edge of the roof top, like burning salamanders trying to consume the entire building. Thunder cracked loudly in the sky as lightening flickered. Charlie looked out over the edge and her face went pale at the sight she saw.

"Oh dear god!" I opened my one eye, the other

had swollen shut. I could hear the concern in her voice.

"What is it Charlie?" I asked, as I looked in the direction she was looking and I felt a knot form in my stomach. The roads around the building we were standing on were completely congested with STAR patrol vehicles!

"Oh shit…CRYSTAL!" With a strange renewed vigor, brought on by sheer fear, I pulled away from Charlie and ran to the edge of the building. I looked down at the street corner where Crystal was jacked into the system, I arrived just in time to watch her jack-out and stare down the barrel of a STAR officer's War Hawk Revolver. I saw, once again in that strange bullet-time slow motion, her reach for her katana on her back. I screamed to her, my voice straining over the sound of the inferno and the booming thunder. "CRYSTAL!!! DON'T DO IT!" But it was no use, she wouldn't have heard me anyway. Not over the sound of the officer's gunshot at point blank range.

"CRYYYYSSSTTTAAAAAAAAALLLLLLLLLLLL!!!! The gunshot and the thunder clapped at the same time and all I saw… was red!"

Remnants: The Corporate Chronicles Book Two: The Raven Spreads Her Wings

Crystal's death hits hard for Raven. Crystal was everything to Raven, friend, partner, sister, teacher, protector, and a lover. With her passing, a darkness awakens inside Raven the likes of which she has never felt but once, in her mysterious dream/premonition. The STAR patrol has no idea the beast that they have just awakened and the trouble Raven is about to get herself into when she takes them on herself. Her psychotic misery induced rampage takes its toll on her body however, leaving her bones and nerves severely damaged from the endeavor to the point where she will need more corrective cyber implant surgery for her body to even function properly again

This pushes Raven even closer toward the cybernetic horror she was in her dream. And what of Charlie? With Crystal gone, and Raven in a fit of despair, what is she to do now? Can the timid little Charlie pull Raven out of her funk? Or will she just fall deeper into that darkness that has awakened within her? And what of Glock? He ran off and left Crystal to be killed by the STAR officers. What will Raven do to him if and when she gets her hands on him? And what is the story with that strange man with Raven's crest? And what about the Johnson they were working for? He had to have known what would happen?

These and many more answers will be revealed in the next book in the Remnants series! Remnants: The Corporate Chronicles. Book Two: The Raven Spreads Her Wings! Coming soon! To a book store near you! Don't miss the continuing Cyber - Punk/Sci - Fi Saga!

9951921R0014

Made in the USA
Charleston, SC
26 October 2011